Smart Cookie

Smart Cookie

ELLY SWARTZ

Scholastic Press/New York

Library of Congress Cataloging-in-Publication Data available

ISBN 978-1-338-14356-0

10 9 8 7 6 5 4 3 2 1   18 19 20 21 22

Printed in the U.S.A.   23
First edition, February 2018
Book design by Nina Goffi

For my mom—always with me.
Always in my heart. Love you forever.

The Greene Family B&B Rules

Because people are counting on us.

Rule #1: Stay inside during a lightning storm.

Rule #2: Stay out of the shed. Always.

Rule #3: Put pantry items back where you found them. Open and out on the counter is not where you found them.

Rule #4: Don't oversleep or forget to wake up on time.

Rule #5: Have the cookies ready and warm for check-in at 4:00.

Rule #6: Shoes. Shoes. Shoes. (As in, always wear them.)

Rule #7: Don't give pets swim tests.

Rule #8: Don't mix laundry detergent with food coloring. Ever.

Rule #9: Don't flush anything down the toilet other than toilet paper. (See **Rule #7**.)

Rule #10: Don't keep secrets.

1

Headquarters, the Cookies, and the Storm

Sometimes to fix your family, you need to keep a few secrets. Even though secret keeping is not a thing that happens naturally when you live at the Greene Family B&B. So if I'm not tucked in my room under the giant Scrabble tiles that say *Frankie Greene Lives Here*, I'm in my once-fort-in-the-basement-now-headquarters with Elliot, my ghost-hunting best friend. Headquarters has rules, kind of like Dad's Greene Family B&B Rules. But here we can be barefoot, keep secrets, and experiment with food coloring. The only official rules are:

Rule # 1: Don't enter Headquarters unless invited.

Rule # 2: Standing outside Headquarters is not the same as being invited.

Rule # 3: Don't knock. We know you're out there.

Rule # 4: Headquarters is and must remain a secret to all nonmembers.

Elliot wasn't an original member but joined when he moved next door. The founders were me and Jessica Blaine. That was, of course, before Ms. Jessica Blaine became my friend-turned-not in the fourth grade. I haven't revoked her membership even though she stopped speaking to me over a year ago. Other members include my puppy, Lucy, my hedgehog, Winston, and Gram. I call them members, but really, they're more honorary guests—they can visit but can't call a meeting. Dad knows about Headquarters but is neither a member nor an honorary guest. He says it's better that way and has offered to feed all Headquarters members. Which I appreciate.

The rain beats against the windows as I grab a handful of cookies to bring down for my emergency meeting with Elliot. This morning, I texted him a Code Red–Hot Chili Peppers after I spent the night awake devising a plan and watching Winston burrow in a sock, eat two yogurt treats, and dig a hole in his shavings. I need Elliot's help.

The cookies are still melty-chips warm.

"These taste great," Dad says as he walks into the kitchen and bites into a gooey cookie from the top of the pile. His hair is brushed, his no-stain white button-down shirt is tucked in, he's got on a belt, and he's not wearing his Middlebury College sweatshirt, so I know guests will be checking in today.

"Thanks." Earlier, I made my famous oatmeal-chocolate-chip goodness. It's my day in the cookie rotation. Gram and I swap days. Check-in is at 4:00 p.m., so the cookies need to be done for the guests *by* 4:00. That's B&B **Rule #5**, right between **Rule #4: Don't oversleep or forget to wake up on time**, and **Rule #6: Shoes. Shoes. Shoes. (As in, always wear them.)** That one's directed right at me. I'm a barefooter, Dad says, just like Mom.

Thunder roars, followed by a bright bolt of lightning.

Dad and I share a look.

He grabs a second cookie to make me feel like the world is a safe and happy place. Then he fills the vase with wildflowers—Mom's favorite.

Another crack of thunder rattles the kitchen door.

He pretends it's nothing, but I know it's not.

"I need to fix the leaky sink in the Yahtzee Room while the Norberts are on a bike ride in town." The Yahtzee Room is peppered with dice and numbers and phrases like *full house* and *two of a kind*. It's next to the Checkers and Chess Rooms, and a floor above Monopoly, Connect 4, and Clue. Don't get why anyone wants to stay where Professor Plum killed

Mr. Boddy in the library with a candlestick, but Dad says it's our most popular room. Something about everyone secretly wanting to be a detective. There's also Rubik's Cube, Candy Land, and the Game of Life, which is Gram's room. She says she's lived the most, so she belongs there.

A bright burst of lightning flares at the window. I gulp a big breath and count to twenty. Slowly.

"Let's leave around four thirty today," Dad says as he pops the rest of the cookie into his mouth.

I nod.

It's Mom's birthday. Every year we have a picnic together to celebrate.

At Weinstein's Cemetery.

2

Just Bad Luck

Mom died in a thunder and lightning storm on her way home from work. She had stayed late to help Professor Kindling with his speech on bats and sonar and something called echolocation. Police said the driver who rear-ended Mom's car had skidded on the wet road, and that was it. She was gone.

No one's fault, just bad weather.

Bad luck.

Bad timing.

I was four. I remember only small chunks of stuff. The smell of vanilla. Her swirly, cursive capital *F* for Francine. And her charm bracelet with lots of puffy hearts that clanked like cowbells when she baked in the kitchen.

I run downstairs and pop open Headquarters' cardboard door.

Elliot's already waiting for me on the neon-green carpet, his shaggy hair flopped in front of his dark chocolate eyes. "When did you get down here?" I ask, handing him the cookies.

He looks at his wristwatch/stopwatch/compass. "Approximately eight minutes ago. So what's the Code Red–Hot Chili Peppers emergency?"

"Sarah Rosen's dad is getting married."

His expression remains unimpressed as he stuffs the entire cookie into his mouth.

"That really seems more like a Code Sweet Green Kiwi," he says.

"Well, it's not. Not even a Code Hot-and-Sour Pickle." I pull back my hair and hope all the rebel strands find their way into my ponytail holder.

Elliot shakes his head.

"I'm serious," I say. "Sarah Rosen's dad getting married means I'm the last remaining student in the entire Dennisville Middle School without a family for the Winter Family Festival Parade."

"Well, um, I hate to state the obvious, but you *have* a family. Your B&B is even called the Greene *Family* B&B."

I say nothing.

Elliot continues. "I think your dad and gram would be surprised to learn after all these years that they're not your family. What will they call the B&B?"

"You don't get it. Sarah and I were the only two who went from a family of three to a family of two. The only two who went from a mom and dad to no mom. The only two who made cards for our grandmothers and aunts on Mother's Day, the only two who learned how to put our hair into a non-lumpy ponytail by ourselves, the only two whose tights always ripped because we didn't know the nail-polish trick. Now, in just a few months, it'll just be me." A dribble of sadness sneaks into my heart.

"Okay, even if I get it, which I'm not sure I do because I didn't even know there was a thing called a lumpy pony or a nail-polish trick, what does this have to do with me?" He picks up a spider from the floor and watches it crawl across his freckled hand.

"I need your help," I say, and then pull out my phone and read Elliot the Connection.com profile I wrote at 2:00 a.m. "'I'm a forty-five-year-old dad looking for someone who definitely wants to be a mom to a great kid named Frankie, a hedgehog named Winston, and a beagle puppy named Lucy, and who can also draw a really good unicorn, and bake melt-in-your-mouth cookies. Search radius: twenty miles around Dennisville, Vermont.'" I stuff my phone back into my pocket. "Well, what do you think?"

"Why unicorns and cookies?"

"I can't figure out how to make a good unicorn horn and think that's one of those things a mom would know how to do. And if she can make good cookies, Gram and I can add her to the rotation."

Elliot nods. I bite my right pinkie nail. It's always the sacrificial one. "It's for his own good. I mean all he does is work and fix stuff."

"If you get caught, this would be way worse than Rufus."

Rufus was my pet snake. I flushed him down the toilet. I thought he'd like it, and I also thought he could swim. Turns out he couldn't, but he could clog the toilets of an entire B&B. For two days.

"I won't get caught. My plan is to post the ad, interview the Possibles, and then have the one we think is best just kind of run into him. You know, accidentally."

"We?"

Before he can object, I hand him a box covered in newspaper. "Here. Happy birthday." Gram had rolls and rolls and rolls of *This Is Your Day* wrapping paper stacked on the couch in her bedroom, but she said she needed it. So I used the horoscope section of today's paper after reading mine (Sagittarius: Make a decision to change what's not working. Embrace something new.) and Elliot's (Aries: Don't start something you can't finish.)

Elliot glances at his horoscope and then rips off the newspaper. The look I had hoped would flash across his round face does. His eyes pop wide, and an oatmeal-cookie-filled-braces smile forms across his skinny lips. "This is total bribery," Elliot says. "You. Are. The. Best. Friend. Ever." Elliot's been obsessed with ghosts and ghost hunters and dead things since his gramps died two years ago.

He pulls the Ghost-Hunter Super-Charged Laser and the instructions out of the box and starts to read, " 'This is the finest tool in ghost hunting. You are ready for your adventures to begin.' " He looks up at me.

I shake my head. "Don't look at me like that. Just because I gave you this thing doesn't mean I believe in ghosts or plan to go hunting for them with you."

Elliot cocks his head and grins. I know that look. "You search for ghosts with me. I'll search for a mom with you."

3

Somewhere Between Dead and Grounded for Life

"Let's try my laser out. The rain has stopped," Elliot says.

"How could you possibly know that? We're sitting in Headquarters. In the basement."

"Lucy has finally stopped running in circles and baying."

I pause for a minute and realize he's right. Lucy's curled in a ball just outside the cardboard door. About a month ago, I found her at Maisy's Florist. Maisy said when she arrived that morning with a bundle of sunflowers, the little gal was curled up in the middle of a boot box. The note attached read *Please take care of her. I can't.*

Maisy already had three cats, a ferret, and a rat named Stan. She said she didn't have even a drop more space to spare. So I asked Dad if we could keep her. Dad was not a fan at first. "You already have a pet. Remember Winston? Plus, we have lots of guests, Gram, and, for a bit, a snake named Rufus."

"Well, the good news is that I already know dogs can swim, so you don't have to worry about a repeat swim test."

A smile crept across his face.

"And I'm not sure Gram or the guests would be happy to be included in the pet category."

"I'm not putting them into the pet category, just the category of people we need to take care of."

"I hear beagles can take care of themselves."

Then Lucy licked Dad's ear.

Now we have Winston and Lucy.

Elliot and I take Lucy outside with us. The air is thick, and my bare feet sink into the muddy ground. Lucy digs a hole in the wet dirt by the garden. I reread out loud the profile I wrote for my dad.

"What kind of mom do you think you'll get with that?" Elliot asks as he slides his ghost-hunting laser next to the picked-over tomato plants in the garden.

"Just regular. Not like Gram old or Maggie-up-the-street young. No one with a skirt that's like casing for sausage. Someone normal. You know, who loves kids. And

11

pets." I step over the no-longer-blooming lettuce, cucumbers, and squash, and remember Dad added "pull dead things from garden" to my list of to-dos. He said, "People are counting on us, Francine, and weeds *don't* say welcome home."

Elliot looks up at me, his eyebrows all crunched together. "Kids? Like you want brothers and sisters?"

"Did I say that in the profile?" A small panic rises from my knees. I didn't mean *lots* of kids. I grab my phone and read over the ad. A trail of ants along the dirt stops like it's waiting for clarification. "It says 'great kid,' singular. Not 'kids,' plural." The ants move on. I look over the profile one more time. I did him proud.

Interests: hiking, climbing, reading, and cooking

Appearance: athletic (more ex-football guy than round pastry chef), brown hair, 6'1"

Family: one great eleven-year-old daughter, one pygmy hedgehog, and one beagle

Occupation: ex-lawyer, owner and chef of the Greene Family B&B—*your home away from home*

I inch closer to Elliot, who smells like beef jerky. The ghost-hunting laser's heat meter hovers at five. It only goes to ten. The one time I watched *The Great Ghost Pursuit* with Elliot, they found a ghost. A dead lady that couldn't pass through until she *saw* her son one last time. The problem was her son died three days after she did. When I asked Elliot how the ghost hunters knew all this, he said, "They just know these things. They're ghost hunters."

I only stopped laughing when I realized he was serious.

Elliot wipes the hair out of his eyes and steadies the laser as we walk past the tree house where I used to eat bananas and peanut butter sandwiches with Jessica when we were friends. The heat meter on the laser starts to rise. "Something's here. I know it."

"You have to stop watching *The Great Ghost Pursuit.* There aren't ghosts just lying around waiting to be found." And by ghosts I mean his gramps, my mom, and Rufus.

"You're wrong."

I stare at him and his ghost meter. In that place in my heart that is echo-empty, I wish he was right. "Anyway, back to the living. I want the new mom to want a kid. You know, *me.*"

Elliot looks up. "And Winston and Lucy."

"Of course." I got Winston a year after Mom died and Dad and I moved from Boston to the Greene Family B&B. He was my sorry-your-mom-is-dead-and-we're-moving pet. The first week I had Winston, he curled into a quill ball every time I picked him up. But now he smells my natural Nacho Cheese Doritos scent and walks right into my palm. No ball. No pointy quills.

The heat-meter needle creeps just above the five mark. "There's a ghost here. I can feel it," Elliot says.

"How can you *feel* a ghost? It's weightless." I crack up. Elliot ignores me and continues to follow the meter toward the shed.

The meter climbs to six.

Mist from the rain dances above the lawn.

I zip my hoodie. I look up at the black sky and hope there's no more lightning. I already know it's a forty-second sprint/one-minute jog/two-minute walk from the shed to the B&B.

The needle jerks to six and a smidgen.

Elliot ignores the sky and winds his way around the large maple tree between the garden and the shed.

I look at my watch. The one Gram gave me when I started Dennisville Middle School. She had it inscribed *Love you, Frankie May Greene*. Gram was Mom's mom. When Mom died, Gram took over.

In a good way. Mostly. Except she snores and has lots and lots of stuff.

"So what do you think? Should I send it?" I ask.

"Well, how are you even going to pay for the ad? It's not like either of us has a job."

"It's free. I mean not all dating sites are, but this one doesn't cost anything."

Elliot looks up from his laser. "If your dad finds out—"

"I know, I'll be somewhere between dead and grounded for life." I take a big gulp of air. "But it's worth it," I whisper.

Then I bite my lip, click submit, and hope Dad doesn't kill me.

4

The Big Red Door

"Impressive," Elliot says. "Now, for your second bold act of the day, let's go into the shed."

I look at Elliot like he's grown five heads, doesn't know me, and has never met Gram. "We can't."

The needle jiggles as a loud bellow of thunder shakes me from the inside.

"We should go back," I say.

Elliot stares hard at me.

"It's not *that*. It's just Dad and I have the picnic thing, assuming it's, um, not rained out."

"Wait. I've got something. And I think it's coming from inside the shed."

"There's no ghost hanging out in Gram's shed."

The meter beeps again. The needle slides to seven.

"I'm pretty sure that wasn't one of the really important things Gram brought with her to the B&B." When Mom died and Dad and I moved here, Gram and all her stuff moved into the B&B with us. Dad says it was so we could keep an eye on her. Gram says it was so *she* could keep an eye on *us*. The only thing they agreed on was that Gram's overflow stuff, all the things she needed to bring with her but couldn't fit in her room, stays in the shed. And I don't think a ghost was part of her overflow.

The big red wooden door begs me to break **Rule #2: Stay out of the shed**.

Elliot ignores the NO TRESPASSING sticker pasted across the door. "If we just *walk* into the shed, we can't mess anything up. No one will even know we were in there."

The needle moves to eight as the sky rumbles with purpose.

Elliot stares at me. "Even the hair on my arms is sticking up. This is what happens right before a spirit shows up on *The Great Ghost Pursuit*. We have to check it out."

Maybe he's right. Maybe if we look and don't touch anything, no one will know. Besides, Dad doesn't want me outside in lightning. That's **Rule #1: Stay inside during a lightning storm**. And, really, this isn't even about me or Elliot's ghost meter. This is about making sure the B&B is safe. What if by some minuscule chance Elliot's right? What if there is some ghost in there? What if it's Mom? I mean not her, but her ghost or being or spirit or whatever thingamajig you call it. What if she came back to be with me? Or tell me something really important?

"Come on, let's go in," Elliot says again, his nose turning red from the chill that's fallen around us.

The needle flutters around the eight mark. He moves a few steps so he's standing right in front of the big red door.

I start to say something, but the hair on *my* arms prickles. I look down and read the meter.

Ten.

I step in front of the door and turn the doorknob.

This. Is. It.

5

The Ghost Meter Never Lies

The big red door doesn't budge. It's locked. Tight.

The ghost meter screams at us.

Ten. Ten. Ten.

Another lightning bolt cracks across the sky.

We run from the shed to the B&B. See **Rule #1**. I wipe my muddied feet across the YOU ARE HOME welcome mat and wriggle my now-cold-and-wet feet to warm them up.

Elliot shakes his shaggy hair. "We were so close. I can't believe the shed's locked. We need to talk to your gram about that."

"Doesn't matter." I say the words, but inside it kind of does. I know what's in there. I mean, not exactly. But, I know it's Gram's stuff. And, I know she wants it private.

Kind of like Headquarters. But it feels weird to be locked out of part of my home. I mean, at least Gram gets to be an honorary member of Headquarters.

"Whether or not we can get inside the shed, I know there's a ghost in there. The meter said so. Maybe the ghost is stuck. Like it hasn't passed to the other side." A broad smile forms across his freckled face, flashing his blue-and-red braces.

I look at my watch. The Mendelsons check in soon. I need to make more cookies and get the special Mendelson Twizzlers out of the pantry. I step over the boxes of new multi-use hangers and baking tins and candles that Gram had delivered to the B&B and drag the yellow stepstool across the honey-colored wood floor. Last summer, I stopped asking Elliot to reach things for me. I'm now a solid three inches taller, though he's somehow convinced himself that we're the same height. I hand Elliot the red licorice, flour, brown sugar, regular sugar, vanilla, salt, chocolate chips, and baking soda that I pull from the top cabinet. I had made a batch of cookies earlier, but Elliot ate about half. Taped to the outside is **Rule #3: Put the pantry items back where you found them. Open and out on the counter is not where you found them.**

This rule happened after someone, who might have been me, left the brown sugar out and open. The next morning, when Dad went to make French toast, the sugar was hard as a brick. He made eggs.

"There's no ghost," I say with a speck of maybe in my voice.

Elliot lines up each box on the counter by height. "The evidence would seem to prove otherwise."

I stick my head in the refrigerator to grab the butter and eggs, but they're stuffed behind the Mendelsons' special hors d'oeuvres. This year, Mr. and Mrs. Mendelson asked Dad to renew their vows since he's now an official, certified online rabbi. I slide the deviled eggs and smoked salmon to the right. "Take these," I say to Elliot. He puts the eggs and butter with the rest of the cookie stuff, then launches into his list of reasons that prove there's a ghost according to ghost hunters everywhere, which somehow now includes Elliot.

1. A ghost meter never lies.

2. A ghost meter rarely reaches ten.

3. When a ghost meter reaches ten, there's always a ghost.

He crosses his arms, waiting for praise for his insightful revelations to pour out of me.

I say nothing. I mix most of the ingredients together, scoop a heaping spoonful of pre-egg batter, and promptly shove it into my mouth. Hands down the best part of making cookies. Elliot rolls his eyes. He's more the crunchy baked-cookie type.

"Mixer." I point with my now floured elbow and yolk-covered hands to the drawer to his right.

"That's all you can say?" Elliot spouts as he hands it over. "I give you proof there's a ghost yards from the B&B and all you can say is, 'Mixer'?"

"A reading of ten on a ghost meter that I bought online isn't proof of anything," I say loudly over the clank of the metal spoon. "Maybe it's a squirrel or a fox or an ant hill."

Or my mom. I keep this guess to myself.

I toss in the chocolate chips, twice the recommended amount, and steal the spatula out of the Trinket Treasure Drawer—started and named by Gram. Every time a guest leaves something behind or gives us a small present, it goes into the drawer. The spatula from Chef Louise sits next to a crystal star from the Reed family, a tiny clock from the Mendelsons, and a little gnome from Mason Hernandez. He told me the miniature ski gnome would bring me luck. I guess if there's a ghost under the shed, then it's not working.

I slide the dough balls onto the tray and pop them into the oven. A trail of flour footprints follows me.

"It's not a squirrel or a fox or an ant hill. The meter only registers human ghosts."

"Says who?" I ask as I wipe away the flour that coats the kitchen tile.

"Ghost hunters everywhere and the meter handbook."

"Then it must be true." I laugh, but inside something pokes at my heart.

"You don't have to believe me, but I'm right. Remember, I was the one who told you about Jameson?"

"Yes, but everyone knew about him."

"Everyone but you."

The first day I moved here from Boston, I met Elliot. He wasn't living next door yet. Back then, that was still Jessica's house. He walked over from his house on Kensington Lane and told me there'd been a murder. I remember it taking me a while to swallow. He must have noticed my face turning the pasty color of snow, when he added the killing was over a hundred years ago. He told me Jameson Gross was killed by his cousin Lloyd Hogan over some property. It was never proven, but the whole town knew it was Lloyd. Then Elliot told me there are only two Hogans still living. Mickey, who's always in debt, and Reggie, a guy who owns a lot of the land and doesn't give out candy on Halloween. I remember thinking that I wished we'd moved to Seattle.

"But that was a hundred years ago and this is today," I remind him.

Thunder shouts through the closed windows.

"That body may have been the first, but who knows how many restless spirits are floating around this town?"

6

Happy Birthday to You

When I think of a birthday picnic, Weinstein's Cemetery doesn't scream perfect place. But for the last seven years, this is where we've celebrated Mom's birthday—me, Dad, Gram, and Mom's headstone.

Today she would have been forty-four.

It finally stopped raining and thundering and lightning. Like the weather gods knew it was her birthday. There are three salami sandwiches with yellow mustard and extra-sour pickles on bulky rolls, one big bag of Nacho Cheese Doritos, two cream sodas, and one root beer piled into Mom's favorite picnic basket. The one with the blue-and-white-checked insides and woven handle that's fraying. Mom used to say it's frayed from love. I think it's frayed because she and Dad bought it like a hundred years ago and it's falling apart.

The first time we came to Weinstein's for Mom's birthday, I thought it would be creepy. All those dead people eyeing my lunch. But it wasn't. It was actually nice in a weird kind of way.

"Francine, grab the other end of the blanket," Dad says as we set up between Mom and Gramps. Gramps was Gram's husband (Mom's dad), Michael. I don't remember much of him, except his shiny bald head and his fake teeth. I'd ask him to take them out and cross my heart that I wouldn't scream. He'd do it, and then I'd shriek and run upstairs. Gram always says, "He was the best man who ever lived." I don't point out that she's kind of insulting Dad because I think she just wants me to know Gramps was one of the good guys. Really all I needed to know was that he always had two helpings of Gram's strawberry banana cream pie. For breakfast.

Gram grabs a handful of chips and walks over to talk to Gramps. I hear her tell him how her best friend, Mabel, cheated again in the last gin tournament at Mills Senior Center and how Mrs. Rudabaker knit her another scarf, bringing the count to five—two blue, one red, one green, and one yellow. Then she laughs and tells him how she's perfected her blueberry bread. I wish I remembered more about him than his shiny head and pink gums.

I turn to Dad. "Did you bring the stuff?" I ask, sitting down next to a big red maple.

He pulls out my sketch pad and a new pack of colored pencils.

Another tradition. Each year I draw a picture while we're picnicking. Dad scours the area for just the right stone, and before we leave, we put the drawing under the stone for Mom. I'm not sure how it works, but somehow I think she sees the picture I make for her.

Mom lays next to Gertrude Levine, *1935–2014 Grandmother, mother, sister and friend,* and across the row is Markus Martin, *1925–2005, Father, brother and son,* and Beverly Simms, *1970–2007, Daughter,* and Nathaniel "Nate" Johnson, *1993–2000, Son and brother.* There's a picture of him with a happy smile and missing teeth on his headstone. I wonder about all of them. Gertrude was seventy-nine, Markus eighty, Beverly thirty-seven like Mom, and little Nate was younger than me.

"Do you think Mom and Beverly are friends?"

"Maybe," Dad says, trying to swallow a too big bite.

"Do you think people like Mom and Gertrude and Markus and Beverly look after little ones like Nate?"

He nods.

"Do you think she's doing anything other than taking care of dead kids?" I wonder about this a lot. While I'm down here trying to figure out life without her, and Dad's cooking, fixing stuff, and taking care of Gram and me, what's she doing?

"Don't know. She used to love to paint, so I like to think she's spending a lot of time at her easel."

I finish a mouthful of pickle. "Should I pose in case she's trying to paint me right now?"

Dad laughs. I love his laugh. It fills the space between us.

"I'm sure she's watching over you. That's just the way she was," Gram chimes in.

I do remember that. Not all the things we did, but the feeling of her. She was like hot chocolate with extra, extra marshmallows after the first snow.

I use the brown and orange pencils to color the damp grass surrounding us.

"Do you still miss her?" I ask.

Gram nods.

"Every day," Dad says.

"What kind of non-Mom-Dad stuff did you guys do?" It's not that I don't know what he's going to say. It's actually the same every time. But I don't care. I like talking about her, and since she's dead, there's never any new stuff to ask about.

"Your mom loved to hike. And pick flowers. So we hiked every weekend, and when you came along, we popped you into the baby sling and you hiked with us." On Dad's desk, there's a photo of me as a little kid with my hiking boots and orange knit hat, and Mom in her matching cap. We're both stretched out across a patch of wildflowers along the side of her favorite trail. Arms out. Legs out. Smiles out. Sometimes I stare at that picture, squeeze my eyes super tight, and try to remember that moment.

But most of the time I just get dizzy.

Dad's still talking. "She was also a great rock climber." He pauses and stares at her headstone. "I was terrible at it." He laughs. "I mean, so bad."

I let the moment hang. He seems to be reminiscing more with her than me. I look at his face and wonder how many people one person gets in a lifetime. I mean, is there some sort of cap on heart space?

"Scrabble," Dad says, interrupting my thoughts just in time for me to catch the mustard that's oozing out of my sandwich. "Mom was a master wordsmith." He says I got that gene from her. He might be right. So far I'm winning our life tournament: 27–18 games.

"And she loved puzzles," Gram adds. "The more pieces, the better."

Dad says, "One time we had a fifteen-hundred-piece puzzle of two horses grazing on our kitchen table for three months. We ate on the couch until we finished the puzzle."

"We should get one," I say.

"You're just like her, Francine." He smiles. "She'd be so proud of you."

I wonder if she'd be proud of me if she knew that I just put Dad on the dating market.

"Love being your dad."

"Love being your daughter."

We finish our picnic, and while I'm shading in the sky, I see Dad putting wildflowers on Mom's headstone and hear him telling her all about me and the B&B and Gram. I consider spilling the beans with her about the ad, Sarah Rosen, and the maybe ghost, but reconsider when I look around and wonder if the middle of the cemetery surrounded by dead people is really the place to have that conversation.

I decide against it and put the picture I drew under the pink and gray stone Dad found.

"Love you, Mom."

On the way home, we stop and get a puzzle.

7

Just Between Us

After the picnic, I hop up to my Scrabble Room. The right wall is covered with a magnetic board and huge tiled letters. Right now they say *Frankie*, *Winston*, *Lucy*, *Gram*, and *Dad*. They don't say Mom. My closet ceiling slants and is too short for most adults. I slide under my quilt away from the renewed storm and open the journal I keep tucked under my mattress. It's eggplant purple and has a butterfly etched into the leather cover. Gram gave it to me when I turned ten. It was my 100 percent favorite gift.

Dear Mom,

Happy birthday. It's weird that I miss you even though I was with you today. Well, sort of.

Dad brought you wildflowers. Sometimes he pretends he doesn't miss you huge, but then I see his sad slip in. Don't worry, though, I have a plan to fix everything.

Except the lightning. No idea how to fix that. I was glad it stopped long enough for Dad, Gram, and me to finish our salami sandwiches, but now it's back. It looks like shards of glass piercing my room. I wish it would stop. Truth is, I wish I could stop being afraid of it. Don't get why I'm scared of it. I don't even remember that night. Not the rain or the lightning or the smell of the shampoo Dad says you always used. You know, Dad still keeps a bottle of it in the shower.

One more thing. Elliot says there's a ghost in the shed. I don't really believe in that stuff, but, just between us, I was wondering if it was you.

Is it?

Love you,
Francine

I read my Mom letter to Winston and Lucy. Winston nods like he's listening. Lucy licks the wings of the dragonfly I drew across the page, catching any remaining crumbs from the Doritos I've been snacking on. I give up and grab my laptop to check email. Not *my* email, but *the* email I created for Brad A. Greene, aka Dad. His profile has already gotten a few hits. I read through the messages.

Bradley,

I assume that's your real name. I much prefer that to Brad. I'd love to meet you. Tea and cucumber sandwiches sometime? I don't draw unicorns, but I do know someone who can make us delightful scones.

Sincerely,
Abigail Lucinda Smith, III

My brain bubble kicks on. Um, no. His name is Brad. No one, not even Mom, has ever called him Bradley. And a scone is not the same thing as a cookie. Ever.

Brad,

You sound great. Need a bit of time. I'm just getting over a serious relationship. Maybe we can meet next month. Or better yet, you could come with me to my support group. They serve punch.

And donuts.

Yours truly,
Almost There

Take all the time you need. No.

Brad,

You seem like a nice man and you're quite handsome. I don't live far from you. Would love to meet sometime soon.

Best,
Georgia

Hmm. Maybe.

Brad,

I don't hike mountains, but have been known to conquer a few laps around the mall. At full speed. If you like older women, I'm your gal. Full disclosure, I'm seventy, but young at heart.

xoxo
Alice

I like your spirit, Alice, but he's got me, his eleven-year-old daughter, so just saying, young at heart may not cut it.

I call Elliot, and we quickly eliminate Abigail Lucinda, the broken heart, and the grandmother. I reach for my Boston snow globe. At last count, I had fourteen snow globes in my collection, but this one is my favorite. I turn it upside down, and the snow sprinkles across Fenway Park. The baseball field and the Green Monster get a sparkly white coat. Mom was a huge Red Sox fan.

"I think I like the third email," Elliot says.

Lucy moves from my lap to Winston—nose to quills. I shake the globe one more time and watch the snow glitter fall. It reminds me of once upon a time.

When I had my family.

Dad. Mom. Me.

I get back to Elliot. "I liked that one, too. How should I reply?"

"Are you free for life and more specifically, the Winter Family Festival Parade this year?" I hear Elliot snort.

"Not funny. I need to sound like my dad."

Elliot's still laughing.

"Okay, a little funny. But seriously, what should I say?" The scab on my hand starts to bleed. Lucy cleans it off, and I put a piece of plaid duct tape over it.

"How about this? 'Georgia, thanks for reaching out. A meeting sounds great. Why don't you come by the B&B on Thursday afternoon for cookies and—'"

"Cookies? No grown-up asks another grown-up to come over for cookies."

"But no grown-up makes cookies as great as you and your gram," Elliot says.

"Even so, we have to say something more grown-up sounding."

"Pizza?" Elliot offers.

"Coffee. Let's just say coffee. All Dad-age people drink that stuff." I edit the email and read it back. "What do you think?"

"That's the one."

For the second time that day, I hold my breath and hit SEND.

Then my whole body exhales.

"So how will you know?" Elliot asks. I hear him chewing what can only be a stick of beef jerky.

"Know what?" I stare at Winston poking his nose in the toilet paper tube I put in his cage and wonder if he misses his mom.

"If this Possible is the one your dad should marry?"

I don't answer.

Because I don't know.

"Maybe you should have some kind of list."

Elliot's got an emergency chore list, a favorite food list, a rotating what-to-wear list.

"That's not a bad idea. What kind of list do you think would help?"

"Maybe a list of questions you want to ask? And then you could have some scoring system for each answer."

"A scoring system? Like in baseball?"

"No. Like you ask if she likes kids."

"Kid. Just one. Remember?" I flip the New York City snow globe upside down. The horse-drawn carriages and people and dogs in Central Park get a dousing of marshmallow white. Gram says I loved when Mom gave me this one. It was a present for something, but I don't remember what.

"Okay. You ask if she wants *a* kid, and then you rank her answer. Let's say the scoring is out of ten. Ten is she's always wanted an eleven-year-old kid named Frankie, and one is she's the wicked stepmom from 'Cinderella.' Get it?"

"Got it." My mind fills with potential questions for my new list.

Then Elliot clears his throat. I always know he has something important to tell me when he does that.

"When I left you, I dug around, and—"

"The ghost is actually in my closet?"

"Close, but no."

I know he's kidding, but I peek in my closet anyway. No ghost.

"Then what?"

"I'm not the only person in town who thinks there's a ghost around the B&B."

8

People Stick to This Place

Days later, Elliot's still talking about the whole floating dead thing. "I know you don't believe me about the ghost, but yesterday afternoon, I had to go to the pharmacy to get some stuff for my mom's stomach. She said it was all wonky from the chili Samantha made for the class." Elliot's mom teaches at Montclaire Cooking School and often says, "Not all people were meant to cook." One time Elliot confessed that his mom may be a better teacher than chef, but then swore me to secrecy.

"What kind of chili was it?" I ask as I hand Elliot one of Gram's melt-in-your-mouth pumpkin spice cookies.

"Don't know. I was going to ask, but then she threw up, so I just left." Elliot stops talking and walking to inhale the cookies in two bites. "Anyway, Mr. Barker from the pharmacy and Joe from Winston Farms were there. Joe had a really bad cough. Before I said anything, they both asked if I'd been at the B&B lately and when I said yes, they wanted to know if I'd heard any strange noises."

"Like what? The BB is old, and the pipes are always howling," I say.

"I know, but that's not what they meant."

"How do you know?"

"Because I said the place is always making weird noises. Then Mr. Barker got real close. Close enough so I could smell the peppermint floating around in his mouth. And he said, 'No, son. I mean strange. Like moaning or floating.' And then Joe said, 'Floating doesn't make noise.' Mr. Barker nodded and said, 'Well, I heard it may be the spirit of that poor dead chap . . .' Then he sorta trailed off, like he knew he shouldn't be gossiping with some kid, and cleared his throat and said, 'Never you mind, just be careful over there.'"

My breath feels spigot fast, so I count slowly in my head but it doesn't work. I can ignore Elliot's ghost meter and even Elliot, but it's hard to ignore Mr. Barker and Joe. I've known them since I moved here. Joe's the one who brings Dad wildflowers every week for the B&B. They wouldn't just make up stuff.

Elliot continues. "I got my mom's medicine and pretended to look at the new *Beyond This Life—Ghosts, Zombies and Their Spirits* magazine so I could hear more."

"What did you find out?"

"That Joe got his cough from his wife, who got it from her mother. Reggie Hogan's real mad about something. Reggie's cousin Mickey owes someone a lot of money, and no one knows where he is. And Mr. Barker can't wait to go home and eat Mrs. Barker's famous chicken parm even though it gives him gas."

Onyx, the Gordons' black cat, crosses in front of us from his house across the street.

I stop walking. "This is not good," I say to Elliot, pulling my Patriots hat down to block the cold from sneaking in through my ears.

"It's just a cat. Actually, a kind of cute cat."

"It's a sign. A bad sign. First Joe and Mr. Barker spread rumors about the B&B and now a black cat crosses our path."

Elliot's chocolate-brown eyes roll upward. The first time he did this I thought he was dying or fainting or about to start foaming at the mouth. Now I know it's his thinking face. "There's no empirical evidence to support the idea that black cats cause bad luck."

"Not everything can be explained with hard evidence." I think about Mom's bad timing, Gram's love of multi-use hangers, and her amazing chocolate, chocolate cookies.

"Most things that are true can be either proven or disproven. Unlike superstitions."

"Well, there's no evidence that there's a ghost at the B&B."

"That's not entirely true. We have the ghost meter reading," Elliot says.

"Which isn't really hard evidence."

"Well, it is if you believe the 2007 documentary *Ghost Adventures: The Beginning.*"

"Which I don't." I blow a big breath out when Onyx makes his way across the street behind Sal's General Store, then say, "You didn't tell Mr. Barker or Joe about your ghost meter, did you?"

"No. But if you don't think the reading means anything, what does it matter?" His curls hang in front of his eyes.

"It probably doesn't, but I don't want them to go thinking something about nothing." There's a speck of me that hopes I'm wrong. Maybe there *is* a ghost. And maybe it's Mom. "For now, let's keep this just between us. I don't want to say things that could hurt the B&B or my dad. Not to mention, any chance with the Possibles. I mean who's going to want to join a family that's harboring a ghost?"

"I'm not sure you can actually harbor a ghost. It just kind of gloms on like a slug," Elliot says.

Up ahead I see the back of Jessica Blaine's sweater and her long, stick-straight blond hair. It's weird how from the back she looks harmless holding her little sister's hand, even nice. But as she walks past Ms. Annie Devlin, our former kindergarten teacher and Mom's best friend, that image disappears like the sandy beach at high tide.

"I hate parrots," Jessica spews at Annie, who's wearing her dangling parrot earrings.

Annie simply says, "Good morning, Jessica." Annie's been the kindergarten teacher at Dennisville Elementary for a long time. She grew up here, like Mom, and knows everyone. Gram says people stick to this place.

Jessica stops and stares at Annie. "It's Jess," she says, like she ate venom for breakfast, then moves along down the path to the middle school. No *good morning*, no *hello*, no nothing to the person who trusted us to babysit Herman, the kindergarten pet hamster, when we hadn't even mastered tying our own sneakers.

Annie doesn't flinch. Her eyes continue to smile as she turns toward Elliot and me. Her long black hair is tied back with a cheetah-print scarf, her parrot earrings are part of a jungle jeweled theme, complete with zebra styled bangles swimming up her wrists. "Good morning, Elliot. Good morning, Frankie."

"Hi there," Elliot replies.

"Morning," I say.

She digs into the front right pocket of her rainbow-striped dress and hands me a small key. I tell her this gold key goes to a brick hideout where the boy named Fitzgerald camps with his pet mouse named Fly. They hide there when they're not fighting Marco, the evil ruler, in the parallel universe of Lazos.

Annie laughs. This is the game she and Mom used to play. Find an item, tell a story. Our story started years ago with a plastic mouse she gave me when Mom died. I named him Fly, gave him a friend named Fitzgerald, and a sort-of-superhero to-do list. Find the chosen one, unleash the powers of the Greek gods, and defeat the bad guys.

"I love this key." I slip it into the front of my backpack. "It's perfect. Thanks."

Elliot and I make our way through the crowded halls to our lockers. Everything in sixth grade is alphabetical, so Elliot and I are always next to each other—Greene and Greer. My locker's decorated with drawings of dragon-flies; his is stuffed with all different kinds of beef jerky: BBQ, black pepper, hickory smoked, habanero, garlic, and teriyaki. I never knew something that gross could have so many flavors. We grab our notebooks and head to class with Mr. Bearson. He's stroking his long beard and standing at the front of the room when we walk in.

Once everyone is standstill quiet, he waves Jessica-call-me-Jess to the front of the room.

"As you all know by now, my family's running the Winter Family Festival Parade again this year." Pause. Smile. I'm surprised when I don't see her doing the parade float wave. "We need everyone, kids and parents, to sign up to help."

That's when I stop listening, wave or no wave. I already know Dad's answer: "I wish I could help, Francine, but I can't. I need to run the B&B. It's so busy this time of year. But Gram can fill in."

I love Gram, but my eighty-year-old, gin-playing, fold-up-chair-toting grandmother isn't going to be nailing, painting, and building our class float. Every year it's the same thing. We bake and everyone else builds. Just another reason Operation Mom has to work.

"Thank you, Jessica," Mr. Bearson says. I wait for her to correct him, but she doesn't. He scratches his beard. "This year we're going to do the parade a little differently."

Now I'm interested.

Jessica-call-me-Jess's head whips around like a possessed demon's.

"Our class will be running a float-theme contest. Everyone will brainstorm themes for the float. Whoever comes up with the most creative and clever idea, wins."

Hands shoot in the air rapid-fire.

Mr. Bearson runs his fingers across his Snoopy tie.

"What do you win?" Shanti asks, her hand waving like a flag on the Fourth of July.

"The winner's family gets to ride on the float with the class the day of the parade."

Jessica-call-me-Jess deflates like a popped balloon. Since her mom's been running the float, her family's been at the helm each year. Her hand jets into the air. "That's not really fair," she says.

"It's good to shake things up a bit. Besides, it's a wonderful way for everyone in our class to be involved in the festival."

Her hand stays in the air, but her mouth stops moving.

I flip and twirl the key Annie gave me between my fingers, thinking about the possibility of riding on the class float as a family.

Dad, Gram, me.

And maybe a new mom.

9

Who Remembers Forever Ago?

When I walk into the B&B, Gram's holding the lime-green tea kettle and standing behind the small wooden roll-top desk. I'm grateful for that desk—it hides the dents in the floor of our reception area where I may have dropped that green tea kettle. More than once.

"How's my favorite granddaughter?" She puts down the kettle, navigates her four foot ten inch body around the welcome center, and goes in for the hug.

"I'm your only granddaughter." I toss my bag on the floor and grab a cookie from the platter.

"And my favorite," she insists as she releases me from her hug that would suggest it's been more than twelve hours since I've seen her last. Which it hasn't.

She picks up a brown box of not-sure-what she's bought online and nods toward the paper in my hand. "What's that?"

Dang. I forgot about the parent sign-up sheet. I'd meant to put it away. Or throw it away. Or shred it into a million pieces. "Oh, um, nothing." I toss it into the garbage.

She reaches into the trash and eyes the paper. "I can do this."

"No thanks, Gram."

"Do what?" Dad asks as he walks in, refills the vase with fresh wildflowers, and immediately digs through the repair binder in the top drawer of the welcome desk.

"Help out with the Winter Family Festival Parade," she says.

Dad looks up. "Oh." Followed by a very loud but familiar silence. This is the part where I wish he'd say, "I'll do it. When's the next meeting?" But he doesn't. He doesn't say anything. Then, after an awkwardly long time of nothingness during which Lucy pees on the floor, Dad says, "I'd love to help, but I'm not sure I can swing it right now. I've already promised the guys at Harry's Hardware I'd volunteer at their annual tool-a-thon, and I told Annie that I'd fix her roof before the snow and ice get here. I'm really sorry, Francine."

Dad's the only one who calls me Francine. Well, he says Mom did, too. But who remembers forever ago?

I nod. I know he would if he could but he can't, so that's it. I get it. My watch beeps. It's my reminder—thirty minutes until Georgia shows up, and I still have no list of questions for the Possibles, which means I have no scoring system and absolutely no way of knowing if she is the right one. I stuff my Dad disappointment into that spot behind my big toe. Figure it's the best place to hide it since my brain is busy, my heart is full, and my back pocket is filled with gum wrappers. I pop on a smile. "I get it, Dad. No worries." He gives me a thank-you look. "So what needs fixing now?" I ask.

"The Wi-Fi in Connect 4 isn't working. Again."

"Try connecting it." I laugh.

Dad laughs, too, then grabs his tool box and heads upstairs.

Gram gives me a suspicious glance.

"What?" I ask in my I'm-not-hiding-anything voice.

"You tell me, Smart Cookie," she says. Gram first called me this after I accidentally dyed all the B&B sheets and towels purple. Well, it was a purposeful experiment involving red and blue food coloring, but an accidental outcome. She loved the lavender flair. Said it gave the B&B a warm, homey feel. Sadly, Dad didn't agree. He spent the next week bleaching away the flair.

"There's nothing to tell." Then I smile and purposefully dive in and eat the last cookie. The Browns are due here soon. That gives Gram one hour and fifteen minutes to refill the plate. It's Gram's cookie day.

"Frankie May Greene, I hope you're not getting yourself into a pickle."

"No pickle here, Gram. I promise." I lean over, kiss her cheek, and grab my bag. I don't have long to clear the welcome area of everyone related to me.

I take the stairs two at a time to my room and dump my bag on my bed. Then I grab my count-down-to-the-parade calendar from the back of my closet. It's tucked behind a valentine from Mateo Fernández from fifth grade, an emergency bag of Nacho Cheese Doritos, and a gold star charm that was Mom's. I slide onto my closet floor, shut the door, grab my butterfly book and my green-white-and-blue-striped flashlight.

Dear Mom,

Elliot says I should have a scoring system for the Possibles. Don't be mad. I think it's a good plan. Here goes.

Love you,
Francine

My list of potential mom questions:

1. Do you want a kid? An eleven-year-old girl to be specific?

2. Do you like pets? A beagle and an African pygmy hedgehog?

3. Do you want to live in Dennisville, Vermont?

4. Do you want to live in a bed-and-breakfast?

5. Can you bake? (Figure I might as well see if we can add her into the cookie rotation just in case a gin tournament and pre-algebra test happen on the same day.)

6. Do you know how to draw a unicorn horn?

7. Do you like to hike? Ride bikes? Rock climb?

8. Do you like the rain?

9. Are you afraid of lightning?

10. What's your favorite game?

11. Do you like puzzles?

12. Are you free the day of the Winter Family Festival Parade?

13. Are you handy? (Things break all the time at the B&B. I already know how to fix a leaky toilet and tweak the radiator so it doesn't groan.)

14. Would you feed Lucy and Winston if I were ever gone?

15. Do you like me?

I'm not used to making lists. Not sure I'm even doing it right. I read it to Winston, who doesn't stop eating the almond-and-avocado mush I made him. I take this as a sign of approval, then shake the snow globe Gram gave for me for my fifth birthday. It has a photo in it of Dad, Mom, and me sitting together on the beach just before sundown. I stare at it and wonder what Mom would ask the Possibles. When I can't think of anything else, I leave my closet and head to the front of the B&B.

It's empty. A good sign.

Elliot doesn't believe in that stuff. He doesn't make a wish when the clock turns 11:11, which I always do while squeezing my eyes shut to block out everything but the wish. And, he almost walked under a ladder the other day on the way to school.

The front door creaks open. Remind Dad to WD-40 those hinges, I think to myself as Georgia steps in.

She looks nothing like her profile picture.

10

Negative Points to the Pufferfish

"Helloooo!" the woman sings in a totally-not-believable Southern accent. Her face looks like the older aunt of her online photo, and her skirt is too short and too tight and too not momish.

I remind myself not to make a decision until I score her answers to the questions on my list. Maybe she's not as old or tightly wrapped as she appears.

"Um, hi. I'm Frankie."

"Well, hello there. I'm Georgia and I'm lookin' for Brad."

"My dad."

Her expression goes from excited to deflated as she realizes she's just walked into a package deal. I guess I got my answer to question number one. I wonder if I can award negative points.

I decide I can.

That's minus ten so far.

"How nice." She glides around the room, running her pointer finger along the top of the dresser. "Do you live here?"

She asks like it's some kind of disease. Another minus ten.

I nod.

She picks up the snow globe the Mendelsons gave dad as a thank-you gift. It's of the B&B, or at least a place that looks like the B&B—redbrick, wraparound porch, garden in the back. "I never saw the point of these. I mean who needs fake snow falling down on a fake world."

I take the snow globe, give her another minus ten, and put it down under miscellaneous.

She sneezes. And sneezes. And sneezes.

I count eight stunted, squeaky sneezes in a row.

"Is there some kind of animal livin' here?" She looks around with eyes that seem to be getting puffier and redder by the minute.

"We have a beagle and a hedgehog. We're pet friendly," I say proudly.

Sneeze. Sneeze. Sneeze.

"I'm"—*sneeze*—"allergic." She blows her nose. Loudly.

I want to say the ad clearly states we have pets, but instead, I just give her another minus ten and a box of tissues.

Then Dad walks in.

It's too soon.

Way. Too. Soon.

"Honey, have you seen my screwdriver? It's not in the box." He's rummaging around behind the desk, barely noticing Ms. Georgia.

"Sorry about that. It's on my nightstand," I say.

"Well, you must be Brad," Georgia says, trying to swallow her next sneeze as she inches closer to my dad.

"I am." Dad wipes his greasy hands on his pants and goes to shake her hand.

She waves it away and sneezes again. "My, you're not at all like your photo. You're even better."

Uh-oh.

Dad doesn't know about his photo.

Or his profile.

Although if he did, he'd be relieved that Elliot and I chose the picture of him I took last spring when we hiked our mountain together. He looks happy and natural. Not like the shots we take every Thanksgiving when he looks like he swallowed his smile with a side of mashed potatoes and gravy.

Dad gives her a polite but puzzled nod and thankfully ignores the photo reference. "Do you want a room?"

Georgia tries to squeeze out a smile before her next sneeze. "I make wonderful pound cake."

"That's nice." Awkward glance.

"So this is your daughter?" Georgia moves away from the desk and stands behind me with her hands resting on my shoulders.

This. Is. Not. Working.

My dad nods.

"Only one?" she asks.

He nods again, and I take a step to the right.

"That's perfect. I love children. I'm not lookin' for a tableful, but one could work."

A tableful?

Dad looks confused. His forehead wrinkles like a sharpei puppy. He's about to say something, until I jump in. "Dad, I, um, meant to tell you earlier. I ran out of hot water this morning."

He turns toward me.

I nod. "Yep. After only like three minutes."

"That shouldn't happen. I replaced the hot water heater last month. I'll check it out." Then to Georgia, "It was nice meeting you. Francine can help you if you choose to stay."

Dad disappears down the stairs. I stand awkwardly in the middle of the room.

Then the door opens again. It's Reggie Hogan, the Halloween Grinch. His burger grease scent gives him away before he even steps into the room. He takes the toothpick out of his mouth and grabs a handful of individually wrapped mints that are for our guests.

"Where's your father?" he asks in a voice graveled from the cigar that dangles from his mouth whenever he's giving the toothpick a rest.

"You just missed him."

"Well, little lady, you tell him I stopped by. Be sure to let him know I need to speak with him soon. It's real important." Pause. His shiny, pointy shoes move closer. "You know, the older you get, the more you look like your mama."

I step back. Reggie grew up in Dennisville, too. But he never left.

Then he turns to Georgia, ignoring her puffy eyes and scanning the rest of her, from her whitened teeth to her pointy heels. He grins and says, "Hello, darling."

She shimmies over to him and digs deep for her best Southern belle performance. "Why, hello there." They make sugarcoated small talk, and Reggie doesn't seem to mind her horrible accent and squeaky sneezes.

"You hungry?" he asks.

"Starving. And, if I don't leave this place soon, I'm going to swell up like a water balloon."

Going to swell up? She already looks like a pufferfish.

"Well, you're in luck. I know this great place a few blocks from here. It's got the best burgers, actual customers, and, hopefully, my cousin Mickey. He owes me some money, so lunch is on him." He laughs and looks around the empty lobby, "Besides, this place is dead." Then turns to me, "Your daddy better do something soon or this here B&B is going to slip right through his fingers."

On the way out I hear him mumbling, "Should've never been his to begin with."

Once the door shuts behind them, I run up to my room. Lucy uncurls from the middle of my bed and trails behind me to the floor of my closet. I flop down with my cell phone, cheese cubes from the guest tray, and my count-down-to-the-parade calendar. The fancy blue dress I had to wear to Gram's eightieth birthday party tickles the top of my head. With a big red never-erasable Sharpie, I cross out Georgia's name from the top of my Possibles list. I make a new list titled Impossibles and write Georgia's name at the top of that one. Then I move to the calendar and count.

Fifty-three days until the parade.

Fifty-three days to find a mom.

11

Mr. Death-Be-Everywhere

"Hey, it's me," I whisper into my cell phone so none of the guests can hear me.

"Who's me?"

I say nothing. With my charcoal pencil, I shade the unicorn's tail in the mural I'm drawing on the wall in my closet. Dad doesn't exactly know about it. Not sure it would make everyone feel at home at the Greene Family B&B.

"Frankie?" Elliot asks.

Lucy tucks her nose under my leg, hoping for more cheese. "Yes. Who else says 'it's me'?"

"I guess no one. How'd it go?" He asks between two huge, frog burps.

"Remember when I made cookies that first time and accidentally grabbed soy sauce instead of vanilla?"

"Those were terrible."

"It was like that. But way worse. Georgia was nothing like her profile. She was older, meaner, faker, and left the B&B with Reggie Hogan." Lucy licks my ears and cheeks and eyelids and nose. It's dangerous to talk while she's full-on face-licking. Her tongue could so easily end up smack in the middle of my mouth. *Gross.*

"Reggie? What was he doing there?" Chewing halted.

I try to speak without opening my mouth too much. "He wanted to talk to my dad."

"Why?"

"Didn't say. Just yammered on about the Drop Bye Tavern being busier, his cousin Mickey owing him money, and how this place should've never been my dad's. Not sure what any of that really means."

There's a long beat of nothing while Lucy focuses on my right ear. It kind of tickles.

"You still there?" I ask as I pull Lucy off my head.

"What if this has to do with the ghost?"

My voice is now the smallest of whispers. "There's no ghost! Your laser-heat thingamabob went off, that's it."

"Put it all together, Frankie. The off-the-chart laser reading, Joe and Mr. Barker asking about moaning and floating spirits at the B&B, Mr. Barker's warning to be careful. Reggie saying the B&B should've never been your dad's. And Mickey owing him money."

"How does all of that equal a ghost?" I ask, smudging the edges of the tail with the back of my fist.

"Mr. Barker talked about some poor dead guy and how Reggie was angry. Remember?"

Elliot doesn't wait for my response. "We now know Mickey owed money to Reggie. What if Reggie went to collect the debt from Mickey, there was a scuffle, and something bad happened? Not on purpose, but by accident."

"Stop! First, no one says 'scuffle.' Second, you've been watching too many episodes of *Law & Order.* Third, Reggie wasn't mad when *I* saw him. He was gross and flirty and hoping to run into Mickey so that Mickey could buy greasy burgers for him and Ms. Don't-Want-a-Tableful. Doesn't sound like Reggie thought Mickey was dead."

"Maybe that was just a cover. What he wants you to think. When really Mickey is dead—"

"And what? Haunting the B&B? That makes no sense."

I look over and Lucy is nose-to-nose with Winston. That never ends well.

"I know, but I just don't think all this stuff happening at the same time is a coincidence. That's all."

I hang up with Mr. Death-Be-Everywhere and log on to Connection.com. Obviously, I need to change my dad's profile. Possible #1 had zero interest in motherhood, me, Lucy, or Winston. I reread, review, and tweak, add *loving* and *family oriented*, then hit UPDATE.

Wait.

Wait.

Read the chapter on *Brown v. Board of Education* for my civics class tomorrow.

Wait.

Answer eight problems on quadrilaterals for math class.

Wait.

Watch Lucy scamper away when Winston crawls onto my shoulder and nose-to-nose turns into nose-to-quills.

Wait.

Then, *buzz*.

One hit on Dad's updated profile.

Hi, Brad. My name is Evelyn. I love kids, B&Bs, drawing, and being outdoors. Want to meet?

Already so much better than Georgia.

I check out her profile. Evelyn. She looks nice. Momish. She has happy eyes and brown hair in a ponytail—without lumps. I message her back and set up a date.

Lucy digs into my garbage can and drags over an empty container of vanilla yogurt. That's when I remember it's trash day.

A year ago, Dad delegated me Trash Kid. No cape. No superpower. Just one smelly job. Every week, I need to empty the trash bins in every room in the B&B and take the bursting bags of garbage to the metal dumpsters outside. I knock on each door before entering with the master key. The second week as Trash Kid I didn't knock first and found a very naked Mr. Reed in the shower singing "Satisfaction" by the Rolling Stones. Thankfully, he didn't see me, but I saw way too much of him.

It takes me an hour to get through all the rooms. I start at the top with Yahtzee, Checkers, and Chess. Then I move to the next floor and tackle Monopoly, Connect 4, and Clue. I skip the Game of Life. Gram empties her own garbage. She says the world has two kinds of people, savers and trashers. She's a saver. Big-time. Dad's a trasher. Finally, I land in our smallest room, Rubik's Cube, and our biggest, family-friendly room, Candy Land. Candy Land has the most garbage. This is the Rubin family's first visit, and their cans are overflowing with lots of paper, juice boxes, stinky diapers, and gum wrappers.

Last up is the lobby and kitchen, and when I finish with them, my four trash bags are heavy and smelly and annoying. I heave them over my shoulders, slide on my rain boots, and run to the garbage bins around back. The dark sky stares down at me. I hold my breath as I open the metal lid. The smell of leftover lasagna, meatloaf, and tacos from the week hits me in the face. I toss the bags into the containers. When I run to the porch to get the rest of the bags, I see Annie across the street.

What she's doing over this way? Her apartment's on the opposite end of town. I'm about to wave and show her I'm wearing the mouse pin she gave me last week, when she pops into her car and drives away.

Weird.

The sun pokes through the rain clouds, so I shuffle Lucy out the door for a bathroom break. We take a slight detour past the shed, and I wait for the big red door to stop begging me to see what's inside. It doesn't. I stand there for a long minute. Maybe there's trash in there that I should throw out. Lucy runs laps around the shed. *Sniff.* Run. *Sniff.* Run. Maybe I should go inside and check. There's no ghost in there. And even if there is, it's probably just Mom visiting. I'm not sure if that makes me happy or sad, but I try the door anyway.

It doesn't budge. Lucy and I turn to leave.

"Still locked?"

I jump back startled. It's Elliot and his death-o'-meter. "You here to check on your ghost?" I ask.

"Hey, I wasn't the one trying to get in."

"It's trash day," I say, almost convincing.

He laughs. "Tell yourself whatever you need to, but I think you're starting to believe me."

Lucy scratches at the boards on the outside of the shed.

"Even Lucy knows there's something in there."

"Some*thing.* Like a dead mouse or rabbit. Not some*one.*"

He reaches out and hands me the metal rod. "You try it."

I grab the laser, partly to see if maybe he's one ounce right, but mostly to show him he's 100 percent wrong. Before I can do anything with it, I spy Jessica-call-me-Jess sitting on the curb across the street, head in her hands, crying. Elliot sees her, too.

"What should we do?" Elliot asks.

I shrug. "The last time I saw her cry was when Sasha Malone stole her Twinkie at lunch in first grade." I've been in school with Jessica since I moved here in kindergarten. Then, in fourth grade, everything changed. Her dad bailed, her mom sold their home to Elliot's family, and Jessica, her mom, and little sister, Leila, moved into an apartment in town. That's when she stopped speaking to me. No explanation. Just total silence.

"Well, we can't do nothing," I say, handing him back the ghost meter.

"Actually, we could do nothing," Elliot says.

I ignore him and call Lucy, who's frantically trying to dig her way into the shed, and the three of us walk across the street.

The moment we're spotted, Jessica stops crying. I swear that's a skill. To be able to stop in under five seconds. That would have been useful when Dad told me we were moving. Instead I cried for two days straight. That's how I know what a pufferfish looks like.

Jessica looks up. Her eyes and nose fight for the reddest part of her face.

"What do *you* want?" Lucy ignores the snap in her voice and licks her face.

"Just wanted to see if you were okay," I say.

She wipes her wet face with the back of her hand, as if she can successfully hide that she's been sitting on the curb crying. "Elliot, you better be taking care of my house and my yellow rose bushes in the back." Anger wraps every syllable.

"Technically, they're not your—"

I elbow Elliot. This is not the time for technicalities.

I just nod. "You all right?"

Silent glare.

In that moment, I wonder if it's possible to hate and pity someone at the same time. Gram says Jessica hasn't seen or spoken to her dad since he left that day in fourth grade. Not sure how Gram knows this, but the senior center *is* the base of all town gossip.

"Leave. Me. Alone."

Her voice rattles me back to the curb.

Okay, maybe it's just hate.

12

No Going Back

"How's this bright and beautiful day treating you?" asks
Annie, a few days later, a smile spread across her face and
a kindergartner stuck to her side. I think about asking
her about the other day, but before the words find their
way out, she digs into her bag and hands me something.
This time it's a pack of glow-in-the-dark stars. They're
all different neon colors, and I know exactly where I'm
going to put them. In my closet above the countdown
calendar.

"This star is Fitzgerald's secret portal to Lazos where
people and pets live forever," I say, pulling a green one out
of the package. Maybe Mom's there. The words dangle
unsaid. I give Annie a double-fisted hug. The only kind to

give according to Gram—"Hug me with both arms, like you mean it."

"Oh, sweet girl, you go on now and have a wonderful day." She holds the hand of her five-year-old shadow, and Elliot and I head into school.

When we get to English class, I see Jessica surrounded by her minions. She's pointing and fake laughing. She looks in my direction, and I turn away, tuck the stars into my backpack, and take my seat.

"Okay, today's Shakespeare day," says Mr. Bearson. "We're going to pair off for a Shakespeare project—and I want you to think outside the box. No dioramas or posters. Consider something online, something musical, something totally unique. Surprise me!"

I look over at Elliot, he nods. *Good, partner picked. Now what can we do that's unpredictable Shakespeare?*

Mr. Bearson isn't done with his instructions. He finishes explaining the directions and then says, "So here's the list of partners."

What?

Before I can raise my hand, I hear him say, "Frankie and Jessica."

My happy-star feeling disappears like Gram's famous chocolate, chocolate cookies at check-in.

We have thirty minutes in class to work on an idea that we'll present later this semester. I slide my chair over to

Jessica's desk. She doesn't lift her head from her unicorn doodle. It's actually pretty good. Even the horn.

"Um. So do you have any ideas for the project?" I open my notebook and title the page *Shakespeare Ideas*.

She says nothing.

"Okay, I was thinking maybe we could turn *Macbeth* into a picture book. It's my favorite Shakespeare play. Gram and I read it together last summer." Gram called it our Season of Shakespeare. She said she was getting me ready to road trip with her to Boston to see Shakespeare on the Common and wasn't sure which play we'd be able to get tickets for. So we read a bunch of the most famous ones. How could anyone not like a play full of witches and ghosts?

Radio silence.

"Or, um, we could do a skit. I could play Macbeth, and you could be Lady Macbeth."

Still nothing.

"Or you could be Macbeth."

Nothing.

I consider bringing up her curbside cryfest to see if she's even listening, but decide to stick to Shakespeare. "Look, we need to work together on this," I say.

Jessica sees the stars sitting in my open bag. "Why do you even hang out with Ms. Devlin anymore? It's not like she's still your teacher."

My glare screams *shut up!*

"She was my mom's best friend," I say.

"So?"

I don't bother explaining.

But she doesn't stop talking, dissecting Annie like a formaldehyde frog. It shocks my insides that from the first day of kindergarten to Columbus Day in fourth grade, Jessica was my closest friend in the world. We used to spend every Friday night at the B&B watching movies, and every Saturday night with her parents at Sami's Bucket counting how many so-hot-it-hurts chicken wings we could eat before guzzling down a glass of milk. Then that thing happened. It was the Tuesday after Columbus Day weekend that Jessica's dad moved out. I remember because we were on a bus for a field trip into Boston to walk the Freedom Trail, when her mom called and told her to go home with me that day. We were excited to have a sleepover on a school night until we found out her dad left and took some woman named Elsa with him. That was the end of our sleepovers, movies, and wings.

The bell rings, and I've written absolutely nothing under the heading *Shakespeare Ideas.*

Elliot and I head to the town library after school. On our way down Leopold Lane, I ask him, "What did I ever do to Jessica? She's so rude. I can't believe we used to be friends. Best friends."

He says nothing.

"I mean *I* didn't walk out on her."

He still says nothing.

"I called, I went to her house, but she wouldn't see me or talk to me. No movies. No wings. No sleepovers."

"Come on, Frankie. There's more to it than that. I mean, I'm not defending her. She's like stale beef jerky, tough and purged of any of the good stuff, but maybe you weren't the most sympathetic friend."

"Not true." I dig into my brain and remember calling and stopping by. I also remember that she refused to talk to me. The day her dad left was like the finish line. Once crossed, there was no going back. To anything or anyone. Including me.

Elliot stops and stares at me. "Did you or did you not say to her, 'Well, at least you have parents. They may not be together, but they're not dead'?"

"I did, but that was, and remains, factual. Of all people, you should appreciate that."

"I do, but not sure she did."

In the library, the hum of the lights ricochets off the walls. Ms. Bradley, the librarian, sends an overly-happy-to-see-you smile our way. I return with an obligatory grin of sorts, somewhere between Gram-you're-hugging-me-too-hard and thanks-I-love-that-ugly-sweater.

As we head to our table near the back wall, Elliot pulls his Ghost-Hunter Super-Charged Laser from his backpack. "Why did you bring that thing here?" I ask.

"I did some reading. Did you know the library was originally the home of the Jacoby family? As in Beatrice Jacoby, who died of a broken heart in her house just two hours after she lost her husband?"

"Why do people say they lost someone? People aren't like keys or homework. You don't just misplace them."

"Anyway, Beatrice died, and rumor has it that her spirit sometimes returns to the library."

I try my best to ignore the monotone tick of the laser. I slide into my seat and see someone's carved *E.S loves J.S.* on the table leg and in the top right corner wrote *Sagittariuses Rule* in black Sharpie. I wonder if E.S. is a Sagittarius. I grab my phone and open our forever game of Word Play. My word has four letters. Before I can tell Elliot how I thought of this word in a dream in the middle of the night, he's checking the aisles for the ghost of Beatrice. When she doesn't turn up, he goes over to the very living Ms. Bradley. He returns five minutes later with copies of old articles on the Hogan family. Elliot's convinced the ghost meter reading, Mr. Barker's warning, Mickey, and all the weird stuff people are saying about the B&B are linked to Reggie, so he's digging into the Hogan family's past for clues.

"I think I've got you on this word," I say, pointing to the Word Play app on my phone.

He ignores me, and the game, and launches into how these articles have lots of details on the Hogan family fights, the hundred-year-old murder of Jameson, and the history of the family land wars. "Frankie, the Hogans have been fighting each other over land and money for decades."

"Okay, now will you just guess a letter?" I smile and stick my phone on top of the papers.

"If I guess, will you help me?"

I pause, wondering if it's worth it. Then I look at Elliot. And the articles. "Fine."

"*A*," he says.

"There's one *A*."

The door to the library opens, and Jessica walks in with her little sister. A tinge of guilt taps my gut. Maybe the freeze between us *is* my fault. She looks my way. No wave, no nod, no hello.

Nope, I don't own this. She's made of ice.

I turn back to Word Play. Elliot goes on to guess wrong seventeen more times, so I win on the four-letter word *jazz*.

"Short but surprisingly hard."

"I know, right?" My insides do a victory dance. Our current game record is Elliot fifty-seven and me, fifty-six.

He slips one of the articles in front of me. I steal a glance at Ice Queen. She's reading *Sophie's Squash* to her sister. She almost looks like she has a heart.

I spend the next hour with Elliot creating the Hogan family tree. I draw the trunk and the branches, and he fills in the details. Who married who, who had which kids, who died and how. At the top we have Jameson and Louisa Gross, Lloyd and Bethany Hogan, Marilyn and Egbert Richards.

They each have two kids who have kids. The married and kids part we get down, but how they died seems fuzzy. There are newspaper articles, gossip columns, and, somewhere buried in there, the truth. The articles say Ned and Mort both died in accidents shortly after the neighbors heard their cousin Red, Reggie's grandfather, fighting with them over the rights to their land.

Maybe Elliot's right.

13

Totally Unprepared

The first thing I feel as I flip my pillow to the cool side is Lucy's wet nose.

"Go back to sleep," I tell her as I wriggle farther down into my sheets.

Her cold nose goes from slight lean-in to full-on nudge.

My clock flashes 6:30 a.m. "Lucy, it's way too early for a Saturday morning." Lucy licks my face in the get-up-I've-got-to-pee kind of way. Which by all her squirming, baying, and nudging seems like it could be right now.

The rain's falling hard.

As I grab my jacket and step into my slippers, Lucy pees in the middle of my carpet.

"Really?"

Then she kisses my face.

I bring her downstairs and weave around a new pile of Gram's boxes sitting in the middle of the welcome area to let Lucy outside. Then I trudge back upstairs to clean my carpet because, after all, people are counting on us at the Greene Family B&B. When Lucy comes back inside, she brings me a soggy toilet paper roll and a tennis ball.

I look out the window and see the sparrows at the bird feeder. Since most of the world is still asleep, I work on the new puzzle for a while. It's a litter of beagles. I put in the last piece on the far right and connect the frame. Now to tackle the cookies. I drag the stepstool over to grab the vanilla and see a slip of paper stuck to the back of Gram's favorite cookbook. It's a recipe for *My Famous Peanut Butter Oatmeal Chocolate Chip Cookies*. I read through the ingredients, and written on the bottom are the words *I love you more than these cookies!* A smiley face with no nose is the only signature.

Mom.

I remember the nose-less smiley face and the best cookies ever.

In twenty minutes, I'm tasting the batter, and in thirty, the cookies are in the oven.

"What are you doing awake at this hour?" Gram asks as she walks into the kitchen and pours herself a cup of hot water. She gave up the tea bag a while back. Now it's just hot water, honey, and lemon. I look at Lucy.

She nods, picks up the recipe and her eyes smile. "I remember these. Where did you get this?"

"It was stuck to the back of *The Baking Life*."

Gram's face goes soft the way it does whenever we talk about Mom. She says loss is hardest when it's out of order. I don't know. I think loss is *always* hard.

Gone is gone.

And gone stinks.

Gram looks at me with warm eyes, "Love you, Smart Cookie."

"Love you, too."

Then she walks over to the boxes. "Oh, great, they got here."

"What is all this stuff?" I ask.

"Some baskets, a few ocean breeze candles, but mostly hangers."

"Why?"

"Why what?"

"Why did you buy more candles and baskets and hangers?"

"I need them," she says, like it's as obvious as putting mustard on a hot dog. "Now, how about some cinnamon French toast to go with those cookies?"

Lucy's ears perk up. My stomach growls a loud yes.

Nutmeg and cinnamon share the air with peanut butter and chocolate. I tell Gram we need to make a room spray that smells just like this. She agrees. We decide we'll call it Baked.

Soon Gram's French toast lines the counter, enough for the entire B&B. I drizzle, then pour over my stack the syrup Dad got from the Lawrence's sugar bush. "Gram, these are amazing."

"They were your mom's favorite." She pulls out the chair and sits down next to me. Her soft hands rest on top of mine.

"Nice jeans." She's wearing the ones I helped her pick out. Thankfully, she took my advice—it was these or a pair with an elastic waist.

"Thanks." Her voice sounds weird. Not scratchy or froggy or gone like when she lost it cheering on the Patriots during the first home game of the season. It's nothing I can point to, just not regular Gram.

"You, okay?" I ask in between bites of my French toast.

"Of course."

"What's with the perfume?" She never trails a scent, and today she smells like the lilac bushes Dad planted next to the shed.

She smiles and says nothing.

"What's going on?"

She moves the wayward hair away from my face. Her hand smells like nutmeg.

"Nothing."

I know this means we're done talking about it, so I give her a hug and text Jessica. I'm not doing this project alone. She can't ignore me forever.

No response.

I email.

No reply.

I call.

Right to voice mail.

Mr. and Mrs. Mendelson join us. "Good morning!" Mr. Mendelson says cheerfully. "Nine hours and counting until I get to remarry my bride!" He grabs Mrs. Mendelson and dances around the room.

"It'll be a great party," I say as I open Trinket Treasures and dive in, eyes closed.

I feel a smooth stone, small clock, pocketknife, ring, snake-shaped pin, bottle opener, deck of cards, and a piece of hard candy (likely from Mr. Rubin in Candy Land—he owns a candy store!). I tuck the sour apple sucker in my pocket for later.

Gram takes a long sip of her hot water.

I try Jessica again. We need a project plan.

Radio silence.

Then a new message. When I look down, it's not Jessica, but Evelyn, Possible #2, agreeing to the plan to meet.

I run up to my room two steps at a time and pull up Evelyn's photo again. With her curly brown hair and nice eyebrows, she kind of reminds me of Mom. Not sure if that's weird.

"Brad" messages her back and confirms the time of their date.

No message, voice mail, return text from Jessica-call-me-Jess. I grab my bag and tell Gram I'll be back when my Shakespeare project's done or at least started.

The apartment where Jessica lives is only a few blocks over. I tug my hat down to cover my ears. The frost from the night still lays across the blades of grass, but the sun's slowly pushing the chill from the air.

I knock, but no one answers. I stand on my tiptoes and can see Jessica in the kitchen.

I ring the doorbell.

No answer.

I call.

Nothing.

Then I push gently on the door.

I'm totally unprepared for what I see.

14

Mix of Blue and Barf Green

The smell of garbage smacks me in the face. Dirty dishes are piled in the sink, macaroni and cheese decorates the counter and the floor, and Jessica's sister cries in her arms. I hear something to my right. I turn and see Jessica's mom, the one who used to make us banana chocolate chip pancakes every Saturday morning, the one who's supposed to be running the float, asleep on the couch. In her clothes. Her hair's stuck to her face and her body imprint on the floral fabric is deep.

Jessica spins around. "What. Are. You. Doing. In. My. House?"

I have no good answer.

"I, um, was, um trying to reach you about the, um, Shakespeare thing." I crack my knuckles and try to think of a better answer. But I realize there is none.

"And when you didn't hear back from me, you decided the next move was to walk through my front door?" Leila stops crying for a moment and rests her head on her big sister's shoulder.

"I'm sorry. I just thought—"

Jessica walks toward me still holding Leila. "I don't care what you thought. Get out!"

Her mom groans, and Jessica's face turns a mix of blue and barf green. She's seen this before.

"Now!"

I step back. "Jessica, come on."

"Leave."

"Don't be like this. We used to be friends. Good friends."

She looks over at her mom. "That was a long time ago."

Another groan from the parental.

"What's going on?" This picture is so far from the happily ever after I imagined in my head. Even without her dad, I thought things were different. Better. Not this.

"You don't get to ask me that. Now leave."

Leila gives me a gentle wave good-bye as Jessica backs me out of the apartment and slams the door.

I sit on a bench outside and take out *Macbeth*. As I reread Act 1, I wonder what kind of creative project I can come up with.

Alone.

15

Dead Guy with a Name

When I get to Headquarters, I check Dad's profile. There's one new message.

Brad,

I'd love to meet you. And I can't wait to introduce you to Nugget, Peaches, Mr. Kazoo, and Princess Pie, my cats. I'm sure we'll all love the B&B.

Signed,
Cat Momma

Four cats plus one beagle plus one hedgehog plus one allergic Gram equals a big fat no. Delete.

Elliot bursts through the cardboard door. "You're not going to believe what I found out," he says as he opens his computer to an entire folder filled with lists dedicated to the Hogan family.

1. Marriages

2. Kids

3. Property Owned/Rented

4. Known Disputes

5. Pets

"Reggie's great-uncle had a marmoset monkey. It was actually pretty cute—big eyes and a white face."

At least Cat Momma didn't have a pet monkey. "What does that have to do with Reggie and the maybe ghost?"

"Nothing."

I hand him one of Mom's cookies. I had packed a couple as sort of a peace offering for Jessica, but they never made it out of my bag.

He takes a bite and stares at me. "These are amazing. New?"

"Mom's recipe."

He gets a weird look on his face. Worry mixed with have-you-lost-your-mind.

"Relax, I don't think she was resurrected to make

me a batch of cookies. Although, that would totally work for me."

His face relaxes.

"I found this old recipe of hers."

He shoves the rest of the cookie into his mouth.

I slump down next to him. My mind goes back to Jessica. When we were little, we'd sit in here and she'd pinkie-swear tell me her secrets while I wrapped her hair into the perfect princess bun.

"Can you believe it?" Elliot asks.

The confusion on my face tells him that I haven't heard anything he's said. I hand him an apology cookie. "Sorry."

"What's up with you? You stuck on the mom-parade thing?"

I shrug. "Brad got a message from Cat Momma, and I just came from Jessica's to try and work on the stupid Shakespeare thing."

"And?"

"I, on behalf of Brad, deleted Cat Momma, and Jessica was just weird." For some reason, it feels like a betrayal to tell him details about what happened when I was at Jessica's house. "So what did you learn about the Hogan family, Sir Sleuth?"

He opens the file and unloads the history of every Hogan family member since the '40s. Their family tree is a cross-pollination of greed and power. Kind of reminds me of Macbeth.

"So guess what else I discovered?" Elliot asks.

"These people are like real-life bloodsuckers?" I make my best vampire face.

He doesn't laugh, despite how funny I am. Instead, he gives me the I'm-serious head lean.

I inhale my vampire face. "Okay, what did you find out?"

"No one has seen Reggie's cousin Mickey."

"*This* is the big revelation? Maybe he's working nights and sleeping days."

Elliot shakes his head.

"Maybe he shut off his phone."

Elliot shakes his head.

"Maybe he's on vacation."

Elliot shakes his head.

"Maybe he's—"

"Dead," Elliot says.

16

Trail of Toothpick and Burger Grease

Elliot says he's working on a plan. I'm not sure I want to hear it, but tonight I'm saved by the Mendelson party. Dad texted me a long list of to-dos that begins with trash and ends with a tray filled with little hot dog appetizers. I quickly gather the garbage and bring it outside to the bins. This time, no sign of Annie.

When I'm done, I pop downstairs. I see Dad's added to the puzzle. The littlest pup has her whole tail. The rooms in the B&B are decorated with twinkle lights, yellow tulips from Maisy's Florist in town (Mrs. Mendelson's favorite flower), and photos of the couple over the years. I like the one where Mr. Mendelson's head is tilted back and his whole body is laughing. I wonder what Mrs. Mendelson said to make him laugh like that.

I pass Dad at his desk. He's on the phone. "Of course. I understand. Maybe the next time you're in the area." He hangs up, comes around, and gives me a hug.

"Francine, you look beautiful." The words wrap me like a warm blanket. "And you need to put shoes on those feet."

I look down and my blue, red, green, orange, and pink toenails stare up at me. **Rule #6—Shoes. Shoes. Shoes.** This one I'm not so good at remembering. I meant to put my shoes on but got stuck cleaning my room (item four on my to-do list) and forgot. I climb the stairs, slip on my uncomfortable, dad-approved shoes with no mud or holes and run back downstairs. Dad shoots me a thumbs-up and hands me the tray of hot dogs.

"Who were you talking to before?" I take the tray and pop a dog in my mouth.

"Just a guest who needed to cancel. Sick relative."

The words swallow the flowers, the twinkly lights, and the laughing photos. I don't know what to say, so I offer Dad a hot dog.

"Not now, but save me one for later. I need to check with Mr. Mendelson to see what time he wants to start the ceremony."

The lobby is flooded with people. Everyone visiting the B&B was invited, plus the Mendelsons' family.

Mr. Mendelson has ten siblings, and all live under two hours from here. Right away I recognize one of the brothers. His one, long eyebrow is just like Mr. Mendelson's.

"Hot dog?" I offer.

Unibrow smiles and takes three. He lines the hot dogs up on a napkin and carefully adds a dab of spicy mustard to each one. "You see," he says, "it's all in the system."

I nod.

"Oh, sorry." He puts his dog system on the end table and reaches his hand out. "I'm Asher, Eli Mendelson's youngest brother."

"Frankie." His hand swallows mine.

"You must be Brad's daughter."

I nod and wonder how he knows. I never thought I looked like Dad. Gram always says I look like Mom, "Same round cheeks, brown curls, and intelligent eyes, one smart cookie, just like your mom."

"Well, thanks for helping out tonight. My brother and sister-in-law wouldn't celebrate their anniversary anywhere else."

They may not feel that way if they knew there might be a ghost named Mickey haunting the place.

Asher wanders over to the shrimp platter. I see him line up the shrimp and dump cocktail sauce on each one. His drench with condiment system seems to transfer to all appetizers.

Gram's serving champagne and smiling. She glances my way and winks. I think she looks beautiful in her navy dress.

I wander around the room handing out hot dogs. The room's packed with toothy smiles and pat-on-the-back congratulations. When my silver tray is empty, I dip into the kitchen for a refill. There are like a hundred more mini hot dogs sitting on the counter.

"I've told you before, selling is not an option."

I look around. The kitchen's empty. I don't see Dad, but recognize his you're-about-to-be-grounded voice. He used it after the purple linens incident.

"Well, you might not have a choice. Soon I'm going to own you and your promissory note. And I'm not as forgiving as that bank of yours." The gravel in this voice echoes through the kitchen.

"You're not going to get the note. The bank will understand. Business is cyclic, that's all this is," Dad says.

"Don't kid yourself, Brad. Your business isn't cyclic, it's in trouble."

The business is in trouble?

"And it's not getting any better. I've heard the rumors just like you."

"They're just rumors."

"Maybe so. But no one wants to stay at a haunted inn."

Chuckle.

Cough.

Chuckle.

I recognize that voice and freeze like an ice sculpture.

The door slams. I see Dad return to the party, and finally exhale. Then I put down my tray and step into the hall.

In the middle of the floor is a toothpick and the lingering smell of burger grease.

17

Code Red-Hot Chili Peppers

The Mendelson party ends around midnight. Long after the mini hot dogs are gone, the ceremony is over, and Dad's threatened by Reggie, I text Elliot that we need to meet in the morning. Code Red–Hot Chili Peppers. I watch Lucy stare at Winston as he weaves around his paper towel roll to his tower of blocks, then to his sock hammock. I flip and turn and flip and turn, thinking about Dad and Jessica. *I shouldn't care about her. She's not a friend. Anymore.* But I can't unsee what I saw at her apartment. Eyes open. Eyes closed. I can't get comfortable. The only thing that distracts me from worrying about Jessica is the memory of Reggie's voice piercing my brain.

I open my butterfly book.

Dear Mom,

Someone at the party said I look like Dad. No one's ever said that before. People have always thought I looked like you. That I have your eyes. Your wild curls. And your duck feet. So tonight when I brushed my teeth, I stared in the mirror for a while holding the photo of Dad at the lake next to my face. Please tell me I don't have his nose. Or his droopy ears. Do you think I look like Dad? No offense, but I like looking like you.

And here's the other thing. I'm scared something bad is about to happen. I'm not sure what to do. I want to ask Gram, but she doesn't seem like Gram lately. She's wearing perfume and maybe even lipstick. And, she keeps ordering hangers and lots of weird stuff.

Maybe I'll ask Elliot about it. Tomorrow he reveals his big plan. Help us both!

Love you,
Francine

P.S. I ate like twenty of those mini hot dogs. They could be my favorite food group. Dad says you used to like them, too.

P.P.S. I'm sort of freaking out about this ghost thing. So if it's you, give me a signal or something.

At 3:00 a.m., I read my letter to Winston. He twitches his nose and I'm pretty sure he agrees that I look more like Mom. Lucy stops listening, snuggles up close, and falls asleep. Sometimes I wish I was a dog. I grab my phone and make a list of the best Word Play words I can think of. At 5:00 a.m., I get out of bed and nudge Lucy. "Come on, girl. Time to find out what's going on."

I slide into my fuzzy-on-the-inside slippers and tiptoe downstairs. There are too many secrets crowding my brain. Time to unearth one of them. I grab a screwdriver and a shish kebob skewer and head outside. Lucy runs ahead, happily chasing the squirrels and chipmunks that are surprised to see us awake so early.

I walk over to the shed where Elliot's meter went off. Not sure what I'm even looking for. A ghost probably isn't hanging out in the shed waiting for me. I mean by now it could be in Yahtzee or Gram's room or nowhere. Truth is, I don't know if I even believe any of this spirit stuff, but something is going on and Dad needs my help.

I inhale deeply to move my brave to the surface. "Okay, here goes."

When I glance at the lock, I realize the screwdriver was a bad choice, so I try the skewer. I saw this once on some crime show I watched with Elliot. My hands grip the lock tightly. The metal's icy. My body feels cold and nervous hot-sweaty at the same time, but I don't stop. I can't. I need to know what's going on. I need to fix things. Lucy gives up on the critters and joins me. I pick at the lock hoping to loosen the secrets hidden inside.

Then I hear a door slam behind me, and my entire body freezes.

18

Empty Holes of Things Not Said

"Francine, what are you doing out here?" Dad wants to know.

I turn around to find confusion wrapped in a navy-blue robe.

My brain searches for a good explanation, but I don't have one. Not one that makes any sense. "Um, Lucy didn't feel well, so I brought her outside."

Half true.

I stuff the skewer and screwdriver into my pocket and pull my sweatshirt down to cover any trace of my lock-picking tools.

"Is she okay?" Dad asks.

"She barfed, and I was going to . . . uh . . . bury it. You know the whole people-are-counting-on-us thing," I say. "No one wants to step in puke." I give him a nod-along-with-me-we're-in-this-together look and hope he buys it.

He stares at me a beat too long, and I think I may need to come clean. I start to wonder what a lifetime of being grounded *actually* feels like.

"That was very responsible of you," he says.

Guilt squeezes my entire body.

"Come inside. Let's get you and Lucy something for breakfast. It's early and cold."

The kitchen feels undeservedly toasty. Dad hands me a plate of scrambled eggs with dill and a heaping portion of bacon. Lucy gets plain rice.

Sorry, Lucy.

Dad sits next to me, breaks his bacon into tiny bits, and mixes it into his eggs. A family tradition. Years ago, I asked why we don't just cook the bacon into the eggs, and Dad said, "That's just the way Pop did it, the way his dad did it, and the way I do it."

I break up my bacon and mix it into my eggs. "The Mendelsons seemed so happy last night. You did a really good job," I say.

He smiles. "Thanks. Couldn't have done it without your help. We're a good team, Francine."

I nod. I know that's true. I'm just hoping to expand our roster by one.

When Dad gets up to make the breakfast for the rest of the B&B, I quietly hand Lucy a piece of I'm-sorry bacon, then clear my plate. "So last night, did everything go as planned?" I ask, waiting for him to tell me what happened with Reggie or show me a sign that everything's really okay or give me the dreaded we-need-to-talk-in-the-library face.

None of that happens. He nods and adds hot sauce to the eggs. I guess we're moving on.

"Where's Gram?"

"Sleeping."

I look at the vegetable clock on the wall. It's 6:00 a.m. "She's usually been up for two hours by now." Actually, she was the one I was worried I'd run into on my mission to meet the ghost.

"True. Hand me the sea salt."

I pause when I give him the wooden shaker, expecting he'll fill me in, but again, he doesn't.

"She okay?"

He nods and reaches for the pepper.

I decide I'll find out what's going on when she comes down to make the cookies. It's her day. I inhale the rest of my breakfast. Apparently, no sleep equals hunger. "Got to run, meeting Elliot." Then the next mom candidate. I leave this part out. Seems lately a lot of our conversations are filled with empty holes of things not said.

"Okay, one thing before you go."

This is it. He's going to tell me what's going on.

"I need you back here later today to make the check-in cookies."

"Why? It's Gram's turn." I grab some bacon for Elliot.

"We just need a hand. Gram's got stuff to do." I think about it and remember Gram said she was on a deadline to get the senior center's newsletter out. Plus, the timing of the cookie making may work out well with Evelyn's "accidental" run-in with Dad anyway.

"Okey dokey."

He kisses my forehead and grabs the whistling tea kettle.

Lucy follows me down to Headquarters. While we wait for Elliot, I pull out my phone, open Word Play, guess three wrong letters, and realize my mind's like a pinball machine on tilt. I can't focus. Lucy isn't having that problem. She's trailing a beetle all over the floor.

"Sorry I'm late!" Elliot hollers as he tromps down the basement stairs. "My mom's emergency list of nonemergency things I had to get done immediately was twice its normal length, and that was before she tacked on feeding Huey and cleaning his cage." Huey was Elliot's eighth birthday present. A very cute, very fat, now very old teddy bear hamster. So old, his fur has actually changed from milk chocolate to baking-tin gray.

"You may be right." I hand him the bacon.

"I know I'm right. I would've been here thirty minutes ago, if it wasn't for the list. How does emptying the dishwasher and folding the laundry qualify as an emergency?"

"I'm not talking about that."

"This bacon's so good. Like a smoky maple. If you guys didn't already have a B&B, I would seriously be discussing the need to open a restaurant with your dad. This stuff is gold."

"Reggie was here last night."

Elliot stops mid–bacon chew. "Headquarters?"

"The party."

"Your dad invited him to the Mendelsons' vow renewal?"

I give him the you're-an-idiot look. "No. He wasn't invited. He just showed up."

"At the ceremony?"

I shake my head. "I didn't actually see him, I overheard him in the kitchen." I told Elliot about the rumor, the cancellations, the cyclic business, and the we-may-be-in-trouble conversation.

"Maybe the person you overheard wasn't Reggie," Elliot says, diving back into the bacon.

"Only one person sounds like his voice went through a meat grinder. Besides, he left one of his disgusting toothpicks and the scent of burger grease behind."

Silence.

"Well?" I see a fly buzz toward Lucy and the beetle. "Say something."

"I told you there's a ghost around here and Reggie's got something to do with it. Do you believe me now?"

"Maybe."

"Well, there are lots of reasons your maybe should be a yes." Elliot's list includes:

1. The ten on the ghost meter

2. The moaning and floating rumors

3. Reggie's threat against my dad

4. Reggie's known lack of heart (I mean, who doesn't give out candy on Halloween?)

5. The mysterious disappearance of Mickey

I then confess my failed mission to meet the ghost at 5:00 a.m. this morning.

Elliot smirks. "So deep down where you won't admit it, you really do think there's a ghost."

"I'm just worried about my dad."

He sits down and pulls something out of his backpack. "Don't worry. I've got a plan." Elliot opens his laptop to a file titled *Dead Guy*.

"Original," I say.

"To the point." He takes me through his elaborate plan.

Step 1: Meet in Headquarters.

Step 2: Bring a box of fresh cookies. Please make a few extra for Elliot.

Step 3: Walk to Reggie's building.

I'm following along until I get to step four.

Step 4: Sneak into Reggie's office.

19

Trust Me

"We can't just walk into Reggie's office," I say.

Lucy has the beetle wedged in the corner and is trying to play with it. She doesn't fully appreciate that the beetle may not think her teeth on its body is fun.

"The plan doesn't say walk in—it says sneak in." Elliot points to Step 4.

"So you and I are going to break into Reggie's office. Unnoticed?"

Elliot nods.

"I hate to bring you back to reality, but we can't even eat the afternoon cookies without getting caught by Gram." It was fifth grade, an early-dismissal day from school. Elliot and I walked into the B&B and the entire first floor smelled like gingerbread. We skipped our peanut butter and jelly sandwiches and instead ate the entire two dozen cookies. I threw up gingerbread for the next two hours and was grounded for the whole weekend.

"But we created an online profile for your dad in secret. And we're finding you a mom in secret."

"That's different." I don't know how, but I know it is. "Look, I've actually got to meet the next Possible in a few minutes. Let's talk later and figure out a plan that doesn't involve breaking into Reggie's office."

"This plan will work. It's the only way to find out what he's up to. And it's not like we're going in with clown masks— we're going in as ourselves," Elliot says.

"Somehow that doesn't make me feel better."

"Trust me."

"That's what scares me."

I leave Elliot in Headquarters outlining the details of our great break-in, while I slip back upstairs. Evelyn's on her way, and I've got only forty-nine days left to find a mom.

My phone rings. It's Jessica. I want to answer, but when I look at my watch, I realize I'm late. I hit IGNORE, run up to my room, make my bed, put on shoes (it's too early to know if Evelyn is a fan of assorted toe nail colors and no socks), attempt to tame my mane with a brush, and fly back down stairs.

"Hello," I hear in the entrance way.

Okay. Don't be weird.

I smile when I see her. She looks normal and has happy eyes. Good signs. That deserves at least five points on my mom list tally. "Hi, I'm Frankie."

"Hi there, I'm Evelyn. I'm looking for Brad."

"Oh, that's my dad." Here it is. The moment when I find out if she's a kid-friendly mom or not so much.

"How lovely!"

Kid-friendly. Plus ten for question one.

"You look just like his photos. Same eyes."

Weird. Maybe I do look like him.

Her glance shifts to the window behind me.

I turn around and don't see anything unusual. Cars. Traffic. Maisy's Florist. I hear Dad clanking around upstairs in the Clue Room. I know I've got about forty minutes of a Dad-free lobby while he touches up the mural of Professor Plum in the library with the candlestick that I may have accidentally-on-purpose spilled cranberry juice on to give myself a little time with Possible #2.

"This is a lovely bed-and-breakfast."

Nice. Plus ten for question four.

"Thanks. We like it," I say.

Then the front door flies open, and four kids come barreling in.

"I have to pee!" the one with curls, a dress, and doll in diapers screams.

"I told her to hold it, but she said she was going to pee all over her car seat," another one with crooked teeth and crossed arms says.

"I wasn't going to stay in the car by myself," a third kid in a Red Sox baseball cap adds.

"You weren't by yourself—I was there," chimes the boy with the book.

Curls hops up and down and up and down. I count. Thirty-three times.

"I'm so sorry," Evelyn says. "These are my children. Kelsey, Jonah, Jefferson, and Jacoby."

Four. Children.

I scan my brain but don't have a question on the list for other kids. Lots of other kids.

"Can we use your bathroom?"

I show her and Curls where the bathroom is, while Crooked Teeth stares at me, Book settles onto the couch, and Cap inspects every statue and photo in the lobby. Dad's a big Larry Bird fan so the downstairs is covered with Celtics memorabilia.

Crooked Teeth takes a big sniff of some wildflowers that sit in a vase by the snow globe of the Boston Commons. "I like your house. It smells nice."

"Thanks."

"I like this snow globe, too. I have one of our old white house with the big tree by the fence. The one we lived in with our dad." He shakes it and watches the snow tumble down.

"Now our dad's dead," Book says, coming up from the page.

My heart fills with drops of sadness.

Evelyn walks back into the room just in time to hear Book. "Oh, I'm really sorry. This is new for all of us," she says as Curls's hand tightens around her pointer finger.

Curls starts to cry, and Evelyn kneels down next to her. "You're okay, baby girl. It's going to be all right. Mommy's right here." The little one snuggles into her mom's arms.

I hear Evelyn take a big breath. The kind Gram takes when she thinks someone's moved the piles of papers on her couch.

"This may have been a bad idea." Evelyn's shoulders sink. "I'm so sorry. I thought enough time had passed, but now I'm not sure any of us are ready for this yet."

I watch her scoop up Curls, gather her boys, and walk out the door. Sometimes only moms can make everything better.

Then I take in all the air my lungs can hold, squeeze my eyes tight, and, in the place in my heart where good things go, wish for a family.

20

Blueberries, Walking Sticks, and the Sun

After school, I meet Dad in front of the school. His Jeep was a Father's Day present to himself. Gram and I got him a Jeep tire cover with a big yellow smiley face on it. Nose included.

"Ready?" he asks.

"Definitely," I say as I hop in and load our music. We made the Climb playlist last year. His song. My song. His song. My song. It takes us to the trail, up the mountain, down the mountain, and back home. I'm secretly hoping he'll tell me about Reggie on the ride, but he doesn't. I think about telling him about Operation Ghost, but I don't.

More conversation holes.

When we get to the path, it's quiet and empty, except for one older couple holding hands fifty yards up. It's beautiful here. The trees, even without their leaves, feel majestic. Elliot thinks they just look naked.

"Here you go." Dad hands me a tall, sturdy walking stick. That's been our thing since I was little and needed one. Now it's just what we do. As my hiking boots crunch against the hardened path, I take in a big breath of mountain air. We walk for a while until I gather all the tiny bits of my courage. "So, um, I was thinking of doing some organizing around the B&B."

"That would be great, Francine. Really helpful. The repair binder is a mess, and the bills are somehow no longer alphabetical, and—"

"I didn't exactly mean *in* the B&B. More like *around* the B&B, the garden, the shed," I say as nonchalantly as I can without giving too much away.

"Well, you can definitely pull the dead stuff in the garden and arrange the tools, bags of dirt, lime, and manure that are left over from the season." Dad takes the left fork in the trail. Most people go right, but we've been climbing this mountain for so long that we know the secret shortcuts.

"Great, and I can do the same with the shed. I mean organize the stuff in there."

Dad stops walking and turns toward me. "Francine, you know the shed's off-limits. It's Gram's."

"That's so stupid."

"Maybe," he says, which totally surprises me.

"Well, if you think it's stupid and I think it's stupid, let's talk to Gram. I can organize her things with her. I won't throw anything away. I mean, it's her stuff."

Dad's climbing again. I see the back of his head shaking from side to side. "The shed is hers. Gram can do whatever she wants with it. That's the deal."

"Well, what if there's something in there that's not hers?" I promised Elliot I'd ask.

"Like what?" He steps on the prickers in the path so I can pass without getting poked. *No blood on my watch* is one of Dad's hiking rules.

I'm not sure how to explain that the thing I think may be hiding in the shed might be the very reason the B&B has more empty rooms than guests these days.

"Don't know. That's why I want to get in there and straighten things out."

"You'll have to ask Gram." Dad stops up ahead, kneels down, and plucks some blueberries and hands me a fistful. Another tradition. The blueberry patch. Hike. Pick. Eat. Hike. Pick. Eat. Save some to bring back for Gram. I wonder if I can barter blueberries for shed entry.

"I'm sorry about the float thing," Dad says out of nowhere.

Kind of shocked he's even still thinking about it. I thought he'd say no, he said no, and I moved on.

Almost.

"I know you're busy. It's okay." I focus on picking the blueberries so the water in my eyes stays put.

"It's not really. It's just . . . there's always so much to do and a lot of people are counting on me. I'm only one person, you know?"

"I know." The unsaid floats between us.

If Mom was alive.

If Mom was around.

If Mom was, well, not dead.

The sun feels warm on my face. I wonder if it's her, Mom. Joining us. Telling us everything's going to be okay.

Then a cloud rolls past, and the sun disappears.

I look at Dad and want to tell him that maybe soon he won't be alone. We'll be a family again. But if I tell him about the mom search now, he'll make me stop. He'll say that he's fine by himself. That he doesn't have time for anyone else.

"Maybe next year I can help out with the parade. I'm trying to make some changes that'll make things better for both of us," Dad says.

"Like letting me experiment with food coloring again?"

He laughs. "Nope. That's going to stay exactly the same. No food coloring. It took me five rewashes with heavy bleach to unpurple all those sheets and towels."

We put Gram's blueberries in the special pouch we always bring for her. She used to come with us until her knee (and hip and back) were too sore for the hike. We climb in silence for a while, lost in our own thoughts. Mine include Gram's blueberry bread, ghosts, and how long it'll take to find another Possible.

"What are you thinking about?" I ask him after curiosity drains my brain.

"Replacing the welcome mat, ordering a new printer cartridge, whether we'll ever actually finish our puzzle, and, how hiking with you is one of my favorite things in the whole world."

And just like that, the sun pokes through the clouds, and its warmth wraps itself around me.

21

Mabel the Cheat and the Caramels

I make the check-in cookies on Sunday—the regular ones—
no need to bring Mom into this today. Then I grab my
backpack, step over Dad's new YOU ARE HOME mat that looks
exactly like the old YOU ARE HOME mat minus the dirt, and
head out to visit Gram at the senior center. Maybe she'll
help me figure out what's going on with Jess and the Dad-
Reggie thing.

When I walk into the center, the smell of cooked cabbage
hits me in the face.

"Hi, Frankie," says MaryKate. MaryKate works the
front desk of Mill's Senior Center and loves Gram.

"Hey there. How'd the paper go?" Last week, MaryKate was stressing over some big paper she had to write for her college social work class, so Gram helped her revise.

She gives me a thumbs-up. "Your gram was such a huge help. Don't know what I would do without her."

I totally get that.

"MaryKate, can I ask you something?" The something that's been squirming around my brain since Mr. Bearson first brought up the float.

"Sure, anything," she says like she has time. Like she doesn't have two jobs and also go to school. She pats the seat next to her and offers me some of her jalapeño chips.

I slide in. "What do you think of the Winter Family Festival Parade?"

She looks confused. "I like it. Especially the hot cocoa with extra marshmallows."

"But, um, do you ever miss not having a family to go with?" Gram told me that MaryKate's dad died from something I can't pronounce a few years ago.

Her eyebrows scrunch. "I *do* have a family to go with. I mean, it's not like before. But I watch the parade with my mom and my uncle James, and I get to see all the people in my life who feel like family. Like your gram and the other folks here at the center who look out for me."

Mrs. Rudabaker nods from a couch in the corner as she pulls on her blue yarn and clacks her knitting needles.

"Yeah, I guess."

MaryKate hugs me and then says, "Speaking of your gram, she looked tired this morning. What's she been up to?"

I have no answer because I have no idea. I let my worrying slide when Dad fed me the she's-busy-with-stuff excuse. Now my worry meter is back on the rise.

The door to the card room's open. I look in but don't see her, so I run to the room in the back where I sometimes find her reading. It's closed. When I knock, there's no answer. A light push on the door slides it open. I poke my head into the room.

Gram's lying on the couch sleeping. Not working on stuff. Not playing cards. Just sleeping in the middle of the day. And snoring. Loudly. I inch the door open wider and put my butt on the uncomfortable mud-brown plastic chair next to the couch.

And wait.

I play Word Play on my phone, win nine and lose four.

She's still sleeping. I whisper, "Gram." I don't really want to wake her, but I want her to be awake. I cough.

Nothing.

I water the limp plant next to the window, then text Elliot, who informs me that Operation Ghost is ready to go. Gram will know if we're doing the right thing about the ghost. She'll know what to do about Jessica and Dad and Reggie. She'll know what to do about all of it. When she wakes up.

I sit and sketch her while she rests. She looks peaceful, which makes drawing her much easier than the time I had to sketch Elliot for art class. He never stopped moving.

My butt starts to numb, so I cruise the halls and land in the card room. This time, Mabel, Gram's best friend, is sitting in there playing solitaire.

"Want to play gin?" she asks. Mabel's eighty-seven and, according to Gram, cheats at cards.

We play anyway.

"A run and three of a kind," Mabel says as she lays down her cards. This is the fourth hand in a row that I've lost. I'm starting to think Gram is right. Mabel smiles, and I see the gap between her gums and her poorly fitted dentures. But I'm just happy she's got them in this time. Last time I visited, she was all gums.

"Good game," I say.

She smiles again and shuffles the cards. "Got time for another one?" she asks, popping a fifth piece of caramel candy into her mouth.

I nod. "Just waiting for Gram to wake up." I'm hoping Mabel will fill me in, but she's quiet as she deals us each seven cards and slides me a piece from her candy stash.

I eat the caramel and continue. "I kind of thought she'd be working on the newsletter. Isn't it due, like, any day?"

Mabel nods but gives up nothing.

I have a terrible hand. No runs, no pairs, no like suits.

"You guys playing cards later?" I ask.

She shrugs. I pick up an ace of spades, put it next to my ace of clubs, and discard my rogue queen. Mabel takes it.

"So what's going on with Gram?"

She stares at me, assessing what I already know. Which is clearly nothing. Then she lays down her cards. "Gin."

"How do you do that?" I mean, I'm not even close.

"Patience."

"And cheating," Ben says from the table next to us. His silver hair catches the sun.

Mabel winks at him. "I bet your gram's awake now," she says to me. As I stand, she hugs my waist. "You're a wonderful granddaughter. Even if you stink at cards."

As I walk back to find Gram, I can still hear Mabel laughing.

Inside the back room, Gram's sitting up with glasses on and book open.

"Just lost too many games of gin to Mabel."

Now Gram's laughing. "I love her, but I told you that she cheats."

I glide in next to Gram on the couch. "So what's up?" I begin. "Dad made breakfast *and* I made the cookies *and* you're not playing cards. So what gives?"

Her golden-flecked hazel eyes hold my face.

"I was up late doing the newsletter. Then I had to come here early to have a chat with Mr. Caldwell. His opinion piece was late again."

"You know he does that on purpose." Mr. Caldwell's piece has been late every month for the last eight months. "He's late so you'll have to find him and have a talk with him at least once a month."

She laughs but says nothing.

"Is that what this is all about? Mr. Caldwell?"

Her fingers wrap mine. "Frankie, I forgot to tell you that I made your favorite blueberry bread from the blueberries you guys brought back from the hike. I snuck a slice this morning. Delicious. I left it on the kitchen counter for you."

Clearly, we're not talking about Mr. Caldwell. I accept defeat for now and grab my book from my backpack. We read together separately until it's time to head back to the B&B. We make a quick stop at Sal's General Store on the way home. I get a double scoop of banana ice cream with chocolate sprinkles and a hot-fudge sundae to go for Dad. Gram buys three frames, four more packages of hangers, and five pairs of argyle socks because they're on sale.

When we walk into the B&B, Dad's pacing and doing that weird thing with his jaw that he did the time I let Rufus out of his cage to play and Mrs. Kohlberg found him in the Chess room, slithering between the knight and the bishop. I think about Operation Mom and the ghost, and cross my fingers that his angry feet and stiff jaw aren't directed at me.

He kisses the top of my head.

Okay. Not mad at me.

Then he asks me to go upstairs. To my room.

Uh-oh.

I hand him the sundae, give Gram a quick kiss, grab Lucy, who's hiding her plastic toy turkey under the seat cushion in the library, and fly up the stairs.

"We had a deal," I hear him say. Dad's never mastered the art of whispering.

"We did. In fact, we still do." Gram's voice.

"Bea, the deal was that you keep the stuff that doesn't fit in your room in the shed."

"Yes, I know."

"I can't have your overflow stuff in the halls or the entranceway of the B&B. It looks terrible, it doesn't make our guests feel like they're being looked after, and, most importantly, it's a fire hazard."

"Okay."

"Bea, they could shut us down. Then I can't take care of you or Francine."

I freeze. The words *shut us down* pierce my gut in a place I can't make feel better. That place where all the really bad stuff goes forever. Like anchovies and Brussels sprouts and Dead Mom.

"So no boxes or frames or hangers or wrapping paper in the entrance." The sound of Dad's voice trails up the stairs.

Wrapping paper? There was more wrapping paper? I could have definitely used some of that for Elliot's ghost-hunting laser.

Gram says nothing.

"Okay?" Dad asks.

"Brad, I'll keep my boxes and things out of the entrance-way. I'd never want to create a fire hazard. But my other things aren't a hazard. They're tucked away in the room next to mine. They're my things, and I need them. I don't tell you where to keep your tools, your repair binder, or your muddy hiking boots."

I wish going to my room meant I actually couldn't hear this.

"Bea, that room you're using for storage is for guests."

"No guests are in it now, and none were in it when I put my things in there. It's been empty for months. I checked," Gram says.

"The guests will come and the room will need to be ready. I need you to clean it out. Or I can empty it for you."

Dad!

Gram's voice slices the air. "You can't throw out my stuff. You have no right. If Meg was here, she wouldn't let you do this. She wouldn't."

At the sound of Mom's name, a big lump wedges into the back of my throat.

I guess Dad feels the same way.

The only thing I hear now is the sound of his boots walking out the front door.

22

Noseless Smiley Face

I dress quickly and knock on Gram's door before I head to school. I have time. It's a late-start day. Some kind of teacher workshop.

I hear footsteps, then the *click-clack* of her unlocking the door. "Good morning," she says as she lets me in her room. A unique privilege. I'm the only one allowed in here. Not alone. But with Gram. She douses her hair with Take Hold—a hairspray created for those living in a wind tunnel or a cyclone.

"I have a plan," I say. "I was trying to make a list of ways to help you, but since that turned into a picture of a bunny, I thought I'd just tell you."

She smiles and gently pushes the hair out of my eyes. "Help me with what?" She stands, looks in the mirror, and puts on the earrings that were Mom's. Silver with a spot of turquoise. She says they're mine when she dies. I told her to stay alive and keep the earrings.

"You know, that thing with Dad. I thought I could, um, help you clean up." I point to her couch and floor and bed, which look more like piles of stuff than furniture. The couch is flooded with stacks of receipts and papers and unopened mail. The bed overflows with heaps of clothes—some clean, some not. I have no idea how she tells the difference. And, the floor's covered with stacks of newspapers. When I was little, I thought she was journalist.

Gram looks around. "I was just about to put my things away."

I stare at my grandmother, then at the piles.

"Honestly, Frankie, don't you worry about your dad and me. We're fine."

"Didn't sound fine last night."

She sits next to me and grabs my hand. Her skin's soft like butter. "Honest, your dad's just a bit of a stickler. And, well, I'm not. But, there's nothing to fret about. I promise." She stands and grabs a brush from the pile on her vanity.

I sigh and edge over to her bedside table to read the framed letter that lives there.

Dear Meg,

I know that you and Brad are moving to Boston tomorrow.

No matter the miles or space between us, I will always be with you. And you, with me. Tucked in that place in my heart that remains yours forever.

I love you, sweet girl.

xoxo

Mom

When Mom died, Dad gave the letter to Gram. He said Mom had always kept it by her bed. So now that's where Gram keeps it.

Next to the note sitting on a stack of books on the nightstand is a photograph of Mom. "Where was this taken?" I don't remember ever seeing it before.

Gram hands me the photo, rolls on her coral lipstick, rubs her lips together, blots with a tissue, and then puckers. She doesn't look tired today. "Found it yesterday. Isn't it lovely?"

It really is. Mom looks like a princess in her long, flowing yellow dress with her hair braided down her back.

"That was taken at her thirtieth birthday celebration. She always loved chocolate cake with chocolate icing."

"I bet if I help you put some stuff away, we'll find even more pictures of Mom. Like a treasure hunt."

"Thanks, Frankie. But, I'm all set. I plan to straighten up a bit in here, I moved my things out of the hallway, and other than that, everything else is exactly where it needs to be."

"Was Mom neat?"

She laughs. "Yes. My stuff drove her crazy, too."

I laugh.

"I love you, Gram."

"Love you, too, Frankie."

Then I give her a double-fisted-like-I-mean-it hug.

I head downstairs for breakfast. Dad's waiting with blueberry pancakes.

"I'm sorry about last night," he says, sliding a plate in my direction. "I knocked on your door when I was done fixing the water leak in the kitchen, but you were already sleeping."

I pour the best-maple-syrup-ever all over my pancakes. The steam rises as I cut into them.

"Everything's fine, Francine."

Why do grown-ups always say that? No kid really believes them.

I shove a forkful of hot pancake into my mouth. "Then why does it matter so much?"

"What?"

"Gram's stuff? I mean why do you care?"

"I promised Mom that I'd take care of you and Gram. I can't do that if they shut us down because of a fire hazard."

"But that doesn't mean you have to throw her things in the garbage."

"Francine, it's junk."

I shake my head. "You're wrong. I was in her room, and she has this picture of Mom she just found. If you'd tossed out her overflow, then we wouldn't have that photo."

His face melts. "Which one is it?"

"She's in a long yellow dress."

He smiles. "Her thirtieth. She looked beautiful."

Pancake sticks in my throat. I stop talking about Mom and Gram. It doesn't go down well with breakfast.

Dad disappears to fix the tub in the Chess Room. Hot is cold and cold is cold. So basically, no hot water. I open the cupboard and decide to make one of Dad's and Gram's favorites—my potato pancakes. I grate potatoes, dice onions, and then blend them together with some eggs. The loud whir of the blender is somehow relaxing. I fill a large bowl with the batter then cover the top with matzah meal. Gram showed me this trick. No measuring needed. I pop in my headphones, open the playlist I made when I wasn't sleeping last night, and spend the next hour frying potato pancakes. When they're done and cooling, I put them on a large plate in the middle of the island next to a note.

Love you both! Noseless smiley face.

23

Detour

After school, I text Dad that I'm going to visit Gram at the senior center. She said she was playing cards with Mabel, but I wonder if Mr. Caldwell will be there, too. She doesn't wear lipstick for Mabel.

I know I should be doing something about the English project, especially since Jessica was out today, but my brain can't share space with Shakespeare right now. I keep thinking about Operation Mom, Gram's stuff, and what else of Mom's might be tucked under all Gram's piles.

Don't feel like walking, so I take my bike. It's orange and black and was my Hanukkah present last year—all eight days' worth in one slightly used ten-speed. I ride down Main Street. The smell of coffee and bacon seeps out from

Mel's Breakfast-All-Day Diner, flooding the air as I pass Mr. Coleman, who's sitting on a bench holding hands with Mrs. Coleman. I wave and weave around the bend, head left at the pond, and pass Stone Family Antiques, where Dad got that lamp that looks like a giant frog's head. I turn at the edge of the Reillys' yard. Pedal fast but not fast enough to avoid the squawk of his backyard chickens.

Then, up ahead, I see a familiar blond braid sticking out the back of a bright yellow helmet. What's she doing here? She's supposed to be sick. She's supposed to be home. She's supposed to be anywhere else.

At that moment, Jessica turns around. I stop pedaling, stare at the ground, and try to blend in with the brood of hens that have come over to peck at my tires. When she spins back around and takes a right at the corner, I begin pedaling again. My breath comes out as white puffs in the cold air. Mills is just up the hill. I reach the parking lot but don't turn in, don't slow down. I keep pedaling. I tilt my head just enough to see her bike climb Lantern Lane. I follow. Don't know why it even matters. Why do I care what she's doing? But I can't shake the feeling that something is very wrong.

At Randolph, I see Yellow Helmet turn right. I follow her, staying far enough behind so she can't see me. She darts to the left and speeds through Mahoney's Dairy Farm. The route we used to ride when we were friends. I know the way. Past the cows, down the dirt path, around the old barn. I wave when I see Mrs. Mahoney in the window. She's beanstalk tall with huge black hair and chin stubble. Jessica and I always hoped someone would give her a home-waxing kit or a razor for her birthday.

Then Jessica heads west on Dudley Lane toward Vine Street. We never went this way. The cold feels sharp against my cheeks.

Jessica slows down in front of a ranch house ahead and stops behind a thick row of bushes, hidden from the front door. The house has black shutters, red brick, and a freshly mowed lawn. Why would she ride all the way out here just to hide? I tuck my body and my bike out of sight. There's a baby boy in a stroller next to a woman sitting on the front steps. Then I see what Jessica sees. A prickly feeling crawls down my neck and snatches my breath. The man who made the best piled-high burgers in the whole world is holding a book, standing just off to the side.

With his new family.

24

No Secrets

Jessica doesn't move.

My heart twists and aches for her. How is her dad here, just a few miles away? And how does he have a whole new family? Gram told me that she heard he lived in Florida.

Out of nowhere, my phone rings. Loudly. It startles me. As I fumble to find it and tell it to shut up, my bike falls over and the chocolate lab across the street starts barking.

I don't look up.

I can't.

Head down, I hop on my bike and bolt back down the dirt path past the dairy farm, toward Mills.

Did she see me? My chest heaves with what-ifs and worries. A murder of crows follows me down the gravel and around the cows. Not sure whether to be grateful for the company or scared I'm in one of those movies that doesn't end well for the friend.

What if she catches up to me? What'll I say? "Oh hi, Jessica! I was in a neighborhood that's nowhere near anywhere I'd normally go and just happened to see you hiding behind the bushes, staring at your dad who's hanging out with his new family"?

I turn the corner, glance back, and see nothing. The crows go east as I turn into the senior center parking lot. I exhale, relieved that I don't have to say anything at all. I slide off my bike and see a woman flossing her teeth in her parked car. Can't deal with dental hygiene right now, so I hurry to put down my kickstand and check my phone. No screaming messages from Jessica. Maybe she didn't see me. A sense of relief washes over me as I head into Mills.

Gram has news. "I beat Mabel just for you, Frankie."

"You have to tell me your secret. Seriously, I have no idea how you do that."

Gram smiles, showing off her lipstick. "I have no secrets."

"Really? Then what's up with the lipstick? And the perfume?"

She says, "Grab the deck."

I look around the room and see Mr. Caldwell playing hearts with Mrs. Rudabaker at the back table. Not sure, but I think he may have just winked at Gram. She looks pretty today. She's wearing the super-soft green sweater we gave her for her birthday last year, which always makes her eyes look like kiwi.

I hand Gram the cards. "So what's going on with you and Mr. Caldwell?" He's still grinning at her.

She smiles, splits the deck, and says, "He writes the op-ed."

"What else?" I ask as I shuffle the cards.

She ignores me and deals us each six. Then she dives into the rules for a new game called continental while barely taking a breath. I know this means I'm not getting any more information about Mr. Caldwell. Continental is like gin, but with seven rounds and more variations. I lose the first two rounds but win on the third and earn bonus points. While she deals the cards for round four, she says, "I know."

I freeze a little bit.

"I know what you did."

Unfortunately, this isn't helping me thaw. My mind catalogs all the secrets I've been keeping. Operation Mom. Operation Ghost. Operation Follow Jessica. Which could she possibly know about? I take the queen of hearts, hoping to distract her.

She puts her cards on the table. Facedown, so I know she doesn't have the two sets and one run she needs to win. Which is a good thing since I only have a pair of queens. "Frankie, I know you spoke to your dad about me."

I lay my cards down across from hers.

"You don't have to worry. First, I'm fine. Dad's fine. We're fine. This is a hiccup. Second, I don't need defending. I promise. I'm stronger than I look."

I know she's right. Despite being four foot ten, she's always been fierce. One time Mabel told me that Gram took on the school board because they refused to allow kids to read *Are You There, God? It's Me, Margaret.* and *Blubber* by Judy Blume. The following year, both were in the Dennisville School Library.

"But Dad had no right to say what he did. Besides, I wanted him to know about the picture."

"What picture?"

"The one you found of Mom."

A tear sneaks down her cheek and lands right on top of the queen of hearts.

25

Partner in Crime

On Monday, I tell Elliot to walk to school without me. I promise to meet him at our lockers with breakfast. Dad got another message, and "he" needs to respond.

Love hiking, sleeping late, unicorns, and puzzles. I also really like beagles and am excited to meet a hedgehog. How fun! Would love to make time to connect with you. Are you free next week? My mom and I could come by for coffee. She loves B&Bs, too.

This is not a bring-your-mom offer. I send a polite no-thanks, move her name to the list of Impossibles and head out to school alone. The wind blows my hair so its usual wildness transforms into full-on Medusa by the time I get to Annie.

"Good morning, Frankie. Not used to seeing you alone," she says, a five-year-old with no front teeth glued to her side. "Where's your partner in crime?"

Given the upcoming break-in, she has no idea how close to reality she actually is.

"I decided to go it alone today."

She cocks her head to the side like she's decoding what's behind my solo mission. Then she swallows me in one of her big hugs. I feel like I could stay tucked in her arms for a while, but Toothless gives me an I-need-my-teacher-back look and I let go.

Annie hands me a stone. It's cream colored and smooth and shaped like an egg.

I roll the stone between my palms. "It's a wishing stone that Larz, a boy from Lazos, gave to Fly and Fitzgerald on their last visit. Legend says the stone has magical powers, but it can only be used to grant one wish."

I squeeze the rock, shut my eyes tight, and wish for things between Gram and Dad to be okay. They both said everything's fine, but the tingling feeling behind my big toes says something else. I think about asking to find a mom and not find a ghost. But if I really only get one wish, I need to fix the people who are actually in my life. I stuff the rock in my backpack and walk into school.

When I get to my locker, I hand Elliot one potato pancake and two cinnamon oatmeal cookies. He finishes them before he even closes his locker and then hands me a diagram. "This is the inside of the building where Reggie works. His packages are usually delivered around four p.m. So the plan is we arrive around four like we've got something to deliver."

"Then what?"

"You go into his office and look for incriminating evidence."

"Me? Why me? Do I look like spy material to you?" I step back. I'm wearing a red long-sleeve waffle tee, jeans, mismatched socks, and Converse. "What about this says sleuth?"

"I'm going to be the lookout."

I lean against my locker. "So I'm just going to walk into Reggie's office and ask him nicely if he knows anything about a ghost, what's going on at the B&B, or the whereabouts of his cousin Mickey?"

Elliot's shaking his head. "Reggie's out of the office all that day."

I stare at him. "How do you know that?" I pause. "You didn't bug his phone did you?"

"No," he says, like that's clear. "He's got a meeting about the permitting for some new building he wants to put up around the corner from Sam's General Store. My dad has to be there, too."

"So we're not really breaking in? We're just walking in?"

"Exactly."

"And this should make me feel better?"

He nods.

Somehow, it doesn't.

When we pass the float idea bulletin board, it's filled with index cards tacked to the board. New England Patriots. Broadway Musicals. The '60s. Ice Cream. Cartoons. Video Games. Pets. Monopoly. Dr. Seuss. Wedding Bells.

"That last one has to be Sarah's." I try not to puke all over my Converse thinking about an all-white float with flowers, a bride, and a groom.

"Mine's the one to the left. Ghosts, Goblins, and Other Creatures of the Night. I thought the float could be a cemetery with tomb stones."

"And dead people?"

Elliot smiles. "Zombies."

I know I need to come up with an idea soon. Mr. Bearson's already told the class he wants 100 percent participation.

My float thoughts are interrupted by the snap, crackle, and pop of Jessica's voice. "So you show up at my house and then ignore my calls?"

"I . . . um . . . had some stuff going on."

Like my gram and dad had this argument, and then I was spying.

On you.

And then I was hiding.

From you.

She waits for me to elaborate, but I don't. Instead I pull my wild mane into a lumpy ponytail.

Elliot chimes in. "Morning."

"You smell like beef jerky," Jessica spews.

"Why, thank you, it's actually teriyaki flavored," Elliot says.

I try to see the girl I felt badly for, but she's hidden under a toxic shell.

For the next thirty minutes, we're paired off to work on our Shakespeare projects.

"You shouldn't have come by," she says.

"I thought it was a normal thing to do. Get assigned to work with someone. Can't reach that person. Stop by her house."

"Well, don't do it again."

My sad feelings for her are officially dead and buried. "Is that why you called me three times?"

"I called you three times to tell you that my life is none of your business. The fourth time I called to tell you to keep your mouth shut."

I glance at my phone and see another missed call from her. "Got it. I won't come to your house, and I won't say anything about it."

"I'm not talking about my house."

"Then what?"

"My dad. I'm talking about my dad."

I look up from my phone and lock eyes with Jessica.

"I saw you," Jessica says.

26

Far from Normal

I feel heat rise from the bottoms of my feet, the ones Dad says are always dirty. My throat feels dry and sticky.

She knows.

"I'm really sorry," is all I can think to say.

She gives me a long, cold stare. "Don't pity me. You're the one following me around. Don't you have friends?"

The insult hangs in the air with my humiliation and embarrassment.

Defenseless, I open my laptop to the blank Shakespeare document like my brain is working. Which it isn't. I pray Mr. Bearson has some kind of English teacher emergency and lets us out early. Which he doesn't.

Then Jessica slips me a piece of torn paper with unicorn doodles down the right side. In the middle of the sheet are lyrics . . . a rap, I think. About Macbeth.

Three witches tell the tale, turn courage to greed.
Ascend, Cawdor, then King, oh thee.
It's yours, Macbeth. The crown, the castle with speed.
The prophecy is meant to be.

Hail Macbeth for his triumph, King Duncan cries.
He shall be Thane of Cawdor now.
Story realized, seeds of darkness and lies.
Macbeth nor the Lady will bow.

Witches prophecy fuels the greed. Feeds the crazy.
Ends in red and daggers. All hail the king.

King Duncan to Castle Inverness tonight.
Dance, drink, and walk the greedy halls.
The crowned celebrates, wholly blind to the fight.
King's dead. Murder stains the white walls.

Witches prophecy fuels the greed. Feeds the crazy.
Ends in red and daggers. All hail the king.

Remove the sons, kill the guards, Macbeth is King.
The witches' prophecy comes true.

Scorched the snake, Banquo must die, Macbeth will sing
Witches assemble, plan anew.

Help is too late. Macbeth's crazy has grown.
Lady Macbeth is dead.
Woods move in cloak of branches, crown on loan.

Witches prophecy fuels the greed. Feeds the crazy.
Ends in red and daggers. All hail the king.

Macbeth and his Lady now colored in red.
Greed, scorn, and treachery, and hate.
Crown returned and witches' tale dead.
Story ends, prophecy of fate.

I read it over. Twice. It's weird, but Reggie kind of reminds me of Macbeth. I bet if there was Halloween back then, Macbeth never gave out candy, either.

Jessica's gum snaps in her mouth.

I look up from the rap. "This is really good,"

"I know." Pause. "I mean, thanks." Her angry voice is slipping.

We spend the rest of the period *not* talking about her dad or her mom or Gram or ghosts. We chew Bazooka gum, compliments of the tub the Rubin family donated to the B&B, talk about Macbeth, the verses, the chorus, and the beat. And slowly things begin to shift. Away from the ugliness to something else, something that reminds me of a long time ago.

"I'm not rapping this out loud in front of the entire class," Jessica says, tapping her newly polished blue fingernails on the desk.

"We have to. Part of the project is presentation. And if our project is a rap, we have to rap." I bang out a beat on the desk. A few eyes look our way. Heads bob. "It's going to be great."

"You rap; I'll make the posters," she says as she clamps her hands down over mine to stifle the music.

"*We'll* rap and *we'll* make the posters," I say as Mr. Bearson tells us to finish up.

The rest of the day, the rap sticks in my head. The count is almost perfect, but the beat's off in the second verse. I play with the words between working on the beagle puzzle. After filling in the last piece of the second puppy, I look at the sheet and read the new verse aloud.

> *Hail Macbeth for bravery, King Duncan cries.*
> *He shall be Thane of Cawdor now.*
> *Prophecy realized, seeds of darkness and lies*
> *Macbeth nor the Lady will bow.*

It works. I switch to the cookies. It's Gram's day, but she hasn't come back from the senior center. I decide to make Mom's cookies again. The smell of oatmeal mixed with peanut butter and chocolate snakes through the kitchen.

Dad comes in with his serious eyebrows. "The Florences canceled. Said there was some kind of work emergency."

"Oh, sorry. You okay?"

He nods.

I offer him a gooey cookie or some of the leftover batter. He takes a spoonful of batter.

"Well, I guess that means we'll have extra cookies." Gram always says, "Stay on the bright side of things, Frankie." But, I'm not sure it's really working.

"True." Dad gives his best fake smile. By now I know the difference. We eat the rest of the batter as silence fills the kitchen.

Finally, I say, "Don't be mad at Gram."

"I was just frustrated."

"But it's her stuff. And she needs it," I say, swiping my finger across the bottom of the bowl to grab the last batter bits.

"It's okay for us to disagree, Francine. I love you and I love Gram, but sometimes we're going to think differently. That's not a bad thing."

"When you're threatening to throw out her stuff, important stuff, it feels like a bad thing."

"Well, we may have different definitions of important stuff."

He kisses my forehead, grabs two gooey cookies, and says he has to run to Annie's to work on the roof for a while.

Dear Mom,

I know Dad thinks Gram's stuff is all junk, but I don't. She just likes to keep things close. Like the letter you kept by your bed. And this photograph of you in a yellow dress. I'd never seen it before. It's beautiful. You're beautiful. If there were teams, I'd be #TeamGram. Just saying.

I also need to confess that I'm a terrible spy. Not sure why Elliot thinks I can pull off a sort-of break-in when I can't even follow Jessica for two blocks without her knowing.

Did you see me following her? Did you know her dad had a whole other family? I wonder about this a lot. Can you see me? Hear me? If you can, will you help me? Everything feels so complicated now. Like runny watercolors. Like I can almost see what's going on but not really. Why can't it be like when I was four and you were here and we were a family? That I understood.

Wish my life was normal, but it isn't and Dad needs my help. I'm his person. I promise, I'll fix things.

Love you,
Francine

P.S. Don't tell Dad about #TeamGram. That's just between us. I don't want to hurt his feelings.

Before I can share the letter with Winston, my phone buzzes. It's Possible #3. "I'll read it to you later, buddy," I tell Winston, then close my butterfly book, and pull up #3's profile. Kind eyes, no kids, likes to draw and hike. Possibly promising. In my closet, I take out the countdown calendar and wrap myself in the afghan Mrs. Rudabaker crocheted me last winter to keep my no-shoes-colored-toenails feet warm. Only thirty-four days left until the parade. Possible #3, Naomi, can come by Wednesday after school. Perfect.

Another *message*. I assume it's Naomi, but it's Jessica. She wants to meet. Not at her house or mine. We settle on the library and agree not to talk about anything but the project. Before I head out, I toss Winston some almonds and grab the trash from all the rooms. Fewer guests equals fewer trash bags. Sadly, this doesn't make me happy. It does, however, make me smell less like leftover meat loaf.

I pull my fleece hat over my ears as I walk down Main Street. The wind has picked up, and I'm convinced the cold air creeps into my body through my ears. The sky is dark blue, so everything is in silhouette. Even Rue and Toledo, the Lawrences' dogs, look like cutouts. I pick up my pace, hoping to warm my insides. It's not really working.

Then I see her.

Annie standing on the corner of Main and Woodside talking to someone I don't recognize. I want to run over and tell her about the picture of Mom. I cough and hope she turns around. If she does, I'll wave and walk over. But she doesn't.

When I get to the library, Elliot's sitting at our table. I wedge into the seat next to him and hand him a crunchy cookie. We play Word Play while I wait for Jessica to arrive. "Possible number three comes tomorrow." I pull up Naomi's profile and show it to Elliot as he takes another cookie.

A burst of cold air whips through the library as the door opens and Jessica walks in. I quickly close the profile.

"What's all that about?" she asks.

"Word Play," I say, getting up.

Thankfully, she lets it go. We move to a room in the back. If we're going to practice the rap, we need space. And a door. I show her the changes I've made to the lyrics. We practice the rap for a while. We talk about Macbeth and the witches and wonder what they'd say about us. When we can't come up with anything that doesn't end in death, we talk about what the costumes should look like. The only thing we decide on are the bloodstained hands. To choose who will play Lady and who will be Macbeth, we break a pencil in two and the one who picks the biggest half will be Macbeth.

"Looks like I'll be wearing the crown," Jessica says post–pencil grab. "And I'll rap."

Together.

With me.

For the next hour, we rap Macbeth and laugh like we used to when we were friends. Maybe the Ice Queen is melting.

Then she asks me for a favor.

27

Two Pieces of Raspberry Bubble Gum and a House Key

I stare at her, wondering why she thinks I'm the person she should be asking for help.

"It's my mom's birthday." Long awkward pause. "I don't usually do the whole present thing, but Leila really wants us to have a real celebration with a cake and a gift." She stares at the radiator on the right side of the wall while she talks.

"I'm pretty sure moms like everything. It can't be that hard." I start to get up. "Besides we agreed. No talking about anything except Shakespeare."

"I know, but this is different. We're not really talking about that other stuff. I just need help. I'm not good at this kind of thing," she says.

"Yeah, but I have absolutely no experience," I remind her. "Why me?"

"Look, it's not that I don't have other friends. I'm not some pathetic loser."

Good to know.

"But you and I . . . we have a past."

"Didn't feel that way at your house on Saturday."

She ignores my comment. "You knew my mom when she made breakfast and helped with homework and acted like a real mom."

Okay, so we are talking about that other stuff.

"Besides, you owe me," she continues.

"Owe you?"

"For spying on me." Her stare hits the floor.

"I don't owe you anything." I check my watch. "But I'll help you anyway."

I wait for her to say thanks, but she doesn't.

"There's a cool store at the corner of Lake Drive and Hammond Way between the library and home. I got Gram crystal earrings there for Mother's Day last year."

I text Dad that I'll be a little late. On the way out, Elliot shoots me a why-are-you-leaving-with-the-Ice-Queen look. I motion that I'll call him later.

When we step outside, the midnight-blue sky has turned black. It takes us five minutes to get to Nina's Collection. Jessica picks up a turquoise-blue scarf. "What do you think?"

"That's nice."

She shows me a frame that says FAMILY across the top. I give her a weak smile and hold up a charm bracelet. "Do you like this?"

She turns it over in her hand. "It's okay."

"It's got a paintbrush, ballet slippers, and pencil." I think it's perfect. Jessica draws, Leila dances, and her mom's an artist. Or at least she used to be.

Jessica glances at the price tag and says, "I don't think my mom would wear it."

The cashier looks up from her phone, fingers her huge silver hoops, and says, "It's on sale. Fifteen percent off."

I smile. Then Hoops says, "I know you. You live at that B&B, right?"

I nod.

"Heard that place is haunted. You see anything weird over there?" she wants to know.

My insides tumble as I shake my head. There's a chance I'm going to throw up.

I look over at Jessica, who, thankfully, put her earbuds in. I trail behind her as she touches almost every item in the store. Vase. Candlesticks. Pins. Perfume. Mittens. Tote. Finally, she says, "I don't see anything in here. Let's go."

"Sorry we didn't find a gift," I tell her as we walk outside. "You and Leila can always make your mom something."

"Yeah, I guess," she says.

We're halfway down the block when Hoops runs after us. "Hey, hey! You have to pay for that!"

I spin around. "For what?" I have no idea what she's talking about.

"You girls took that charm bracelet. You can't just walk out with it. You have to pay for it."

"We didn't walk out with anything," I say. There are so many reasons why I'm never going into that store again.

Jessica says nothing.

"I need you to empty your pockets," Hoops says.

Jessica takes everything out of her jeans. Two pieces of raspberry bubble gum and a house key.

I turn out my jacket pockets.

The charm bracelet falls onto the pavement.

28

Dripping with Lies

I stare at the bracelet. Shock pierces my body. Hoops marches over and picks it off the sidewalk. She points her newly manicured finger in my face. "I should call the police." She grabs her cell phone out of the pocket of her too-tight jeans. It takes a slow minute.

Jessica places her manicured hand on Hoops's arm. "Oh, please don't. My friend didn't mean to take it. I swear."

"Let me guess. It was the ghost," Hoops says, staring at me.

I say nothing. My brain races. Mad flushes through my veins and stifles any coherent thought.

Jessica whispers, "She's got a problem and is getting help. This was her first shopping outing in a long time. I guess it was too soon. We're truly sorry."

What? I can't believe the story she's weaving about me. I'm now apparently a recovering kleptomaniac.

Hoops tucks her phone back into her pocket, so at least I won't have to face the police. "I don't want to see you girls in the store ever again." She turns away, her black boots smacking the pavement as she goes.

I storm down the street away from Jessica. My jaw throbs from clenching my teeth. *Why did I believe her? I'm such an idiot.* Every word out of her mouth is a lie.

Jessica catches up to me. "Don't be mad. The clerk was texting the whole time we were in the store. I never thought we'd get caught."

"Make a card for your mom and leave me alone."

"You have to believe me."

I stop and stare at her dripping with lies. "I don't *have* to believe you. You used me. You said you wanted my help. You lied. You stole that jewelry and put it in my pocket! *My* pocket!"

"Leila wants a birthday party like we used to have when we were family. I panicked when I saw how expensive everything was."

"You're lying."

"I'm not."

"If you really thought you wouldn't get caught, then why didn't you put the bracelet in your own pocket?"

Silence.

At school, I avoid Jessica like the bubonic plague. They're both painful and toxic. I tell her to practice. Alone. After school, I head to the senior center. The shades are closed in the reading room and Gram's sleeping. I realize that Mills is the place for random nappers. On the way in, I passed JJ sound asleep in the hall. Gram's snoring. I water the plants in the room, draw her another picture of a dragonfly, and then sit with her.

"So, Gram, you're never going to believe what's going on." I proceed to tell Sleeping Gram everything that's happened with Jessica, the ghost, and Dad. "I'm a bit worried about him," I tell her. "Business is slow. Don't ask how I know that. It has to do with mini hot dogs, a toothpick, and burger grease. Plus, he's doing that thing with his jaw again. I know you know what I'm talking about."

I take a breath to see if she's still sleeping. If she's not, I need to stop talking.

Snore.

"Okay, here's the other thing. If I'm being completely-spill-the-beans honest, I'm kind of trying to get Dad a new wife. Now before you tell me I shouldn't stick my nose in anyone else's business, I really think he needs to do something other than fix toilets and repaint and cook."

Knock. Knock.

Mabel pokes her head in. "Hey, want to play cards until Sleeping Beauty wakes up?"

I grab Gram's deck and follow Mabel to the room down the hall. Barney, Ida, Rachel, and José are playing bridge in the corner.

Mabel leans into me real close. "That Ida's a cheater." I laugh as she takes off her red velour zip jacket and deals us each seven cards.

I organize my cards and hope I can win at least one game. "So what's going on with Gram?"

Mabel looks at me and says nothing.

"You can tell me this stuff. I mean, I'm her granddaughter. And even though I'm eleven, Dad says I'm mature for my age." I discard the six of clubs and slide the two of hearts into my hand next to the three of hearts.

"It's not for me to say." She takes my six and hands me three caramel candies. Then she rearranges her cards and says, "Gin."

Over the next hour, I win one game off Mabel and consider it a victory, even though she wins seven and tells me absolutely nothing about Gram.

Afterward, I walk back to see if Gram is awake. It takes me a quick minute to process her newly applied coral lipstick. I hug her and we talk about Mabel and my card strategy, which is nothing but luck disguised as a plan.

Then there's a knock on the door. It's Mr. Caldwell. In a suit. And a red-and-navy-blue-striped tie.

He's smiling.

"Sid, this is my granddaughter, Frankie."

Sid? When did he stop being Mr. Caldwell?

He shakes my hand. He's a solid six feet tall with absolutely no hair. "So nice to meet you," he says. "Your gram's told me so much about you."

"Really?" *She's told me nothing about you.*

"Sid and I have been spending a lot of time together," Gram says.

Mr. Caldwell winks at Gram.

This is it. Gram's secret. She hasn't been working long hours on the paper and isn't sick with some rare disease, she's just been here with Sid.

Most of me is happy. But there's a small speck of me that wonders if I just lost a piece of my gram to a (nice) old bald man.

"Your gram is quite a card player," Sid says through a gooey grin.

"Not as good as me," Mabel says as she walks into the room.

"That's because I don't cheat," Gram says.

"Tell yourself whatever you want, Bea. But I'm the one with the winning record." Mabel pops another caramel candy into her mouth, and they all laugh.

I look at Gram. She's happy. Like birthday-morning kind of happy.

We sit like this for a while, and then Gram and I make our way back to the B&B. On the way home, we talk about Sid/Mr. Caldwell. Gram's eyes smile when she tells me that he likes horror movies, green tomatoes, pastrami, and reading the last page of a book first. Then she says she needs to pick up a few things at the yard sale on Spaulding Lane. For Sid.

Gram's old stuff I can defend. But being with Gram when she buys someone else's old stuff somehow feels like I'm betraying Dad.

I wait in the car.

29

Snow Day

When I roll over, my clock's flashing 9:00 a.m. I lay in bed for half a second until I realize that I'm late for school, I missed my pre-algebra quiz, and Lucy's peed on my floor. I whip the covers off, toss on my pink fuzzy slippers, and run downstairs, trying hard not to knock over Mr. Hernandez on the landing.

"Why didn't you wake me?" I demand as I burst into the kitchen, where Dad's cleaning up breakfast.

"First, good morning. Second, you wake you. Third, you have a snow day."

I run to the window. A solid twelve inches of fresh snow coats the lawn. A zip of happiness sprints through my body. I hug Dad, steal a piece of bacon, and run back upstairs.

I sink just a bit when I remember the puddle on my floor. I'm about to yell at Lucy when I see her hiding behind my nightstand with her head hanging low and her tail tucked between her legs.

"Okay. You're too cute to be mad at, but you've got to figure out a way to wake me when you need to pee. Okay?" She tips her head to the right. "I'll take that as a yes."

After I clean my carpet, Dad hands me more bacon and a heaping plate of scrambled eggs. "What's in these? They're amazing," I say, scooping up a big forkful of eggs.

"Ah. Used some of the truffle salt Gram bought last month."

"Do you know that she's dating Mr. Caldwell?"

Dad nods. "She told me the first time he took her to Armin's Villa for dinner. I hadn't seen her that happy since Mom."

Was alive floats unsaid.

I finish my eggs and head to the sink. "You want me to wash or dry?"

"The dishes are all done. You're off the hook today. A true snow day."

Confusion sets in. I look around. Usually the kitchen isn't clean from breakfast until closer to lunch. I slept late but not that late.

"Only the Hernandez family and Mendelsons are still here."

"Where's everyone else?"

"The Florences canceled for work, the Herraras had a family emergency, and the Lings' car broke down. I don't remember why the others canceled."

The word *ghost* sticks in my throat. This has never happened before. Never. The one person who would know what to say is Gram and she's with Sid. "I, um, I'm sorry."

Stupid thing to say.

I want to take it back. But, I can't.

"It's okay, Francine. No worries." He winks at me the way he did after he'd check under my bed when I was five and promise me that Ned, the one-eyed monster who I believed lived there, had packed up and moved away.

"This happens. Business is cyclic."

That's what he said to Reggie, but I don't believe him. The empty rooms outnumber the ones with guests. Dad's voice says no worries, but the vacant B&B screams the opposite.

He interrupts my rising worry meter. "I'm heading to the store to get more sand for the driveway, and then I told Annie and Maisy I'd stop by with the snow blower and clear their driveways."

"Are we still hiking later today?" I ask. It's our day.

"Oh, sweetie, with all the snow, I still have so much to do around here. Shovel the front. Shovel the back. Put down the sand. Clear the sidewalk so the B&B is safe for all of our guests."

In the past, once we put "hiking" on the calendar, it was there for good. No canceling. Snow or no snow. I stuff my hint of disappointment behind my big toe. "I get it. People are counting on us," I say.

"Exactly." He nods, then kisses my head and leaves. More determined than ever, I text Naomi. Want to see if she can come early since I don't have school, Dad's out, and apparently, we're not hiking.

She replies immediately. She can be here in thirty minutes. She has a truck and is already dug out of her driveway.

I look down and see that I'm still wearing my fuzzy slippers, so I run back to my room to make myself look like someone Possible #3 could love. I start by trying to tame the beast that is my hair and finish by putting shoes on my feet. Nice, no-holes-in-them shoes. Actually green sneakers but, still, no holes.

Thirty minutes later, the front door creaks open and standing there is Naomi.

A much older version of the woman in her profile picture. I wonder if Dad's the only one with a recent photograph of himself.

"Hi," she says. "I'm looking for Brad." She smiles.

Nice teeth. That's positive.

"He actually had to run out. At the last minute."

She looks disappointed, and I feel kind of bad. I want to tell her it's for everyone's benefit that she meets me first. But it feels too complicated to explain.

"I'm Frankie. Brad's daughter."

She gives me a warm smile. That's ten points in her favor. I bring over the leftover cranberry muffins from this morning. "He made these. You should try one. He's a really good baker. And cook."

She takes a bite, and I can tell by her soft groan that she agrees.

"Do you bake, too?"

She's interested in me. That's another plus ten.

"Yep. I'm on cookie detail half the time," I say, pointing to the check-in platter. "The other times my gram makes them."

"What else do you like to do?" she asks, reaching for another muffin. I notice a long scar down the side of her arm.

"Draw." *And recently, I've taken up spying.*

"Charcoal? Pencil?" she wants to know.

"I love charcoal." Even though I've already eaten enough bacon to fill a grown man's belly, I grab a muffin. They smell too good to ignore.

"I used to teach art at the community college."

"Cool. Why did you stop?"

She doesn't answer right away. Then she points to the long red line running down her arm. "Had to deal with some medical stuff."

I wonder if she was in a car accident on a rainy night.

"Once they put Humpty Dumpty back together again, I just felt like exploring other things."

"Like what?" I ask.

"Well, I still draw. Just don't teach it. I took up hiking in the summer and snow shoeing in the winter. I found I love everything about the outdoors."

"Me too. I like to hike up Gale Mountain to Beaver Creek and draw sitting on the big boulder next to the row of trees. It's one of my favorite spots."

"I'll have to explore that route some time." She glances at her watch.

I don't know what to do. I mean I like her. I do. But the way I like Mabel.

"Do you think your dad will be back soon?"

I'm about to say no when the door opens.

It's Dad.

30

One More Day

Naomi stands and walks over to Dad.

Uh-oh.

My brain's screaming Code Red–Hot Chili Peppers! Code Red–Hot Chili Peppers!

"Hi, I'm Naomi." I notice her scar again. I think about the scar on my chin from the time I fell on the driveway—facedown—after an ice storm. I wonder if Mom would have had a scar.

Dad smiles politely. "You look familiar," he says.

"You too. I thought so when I first saw your picture."

I hold my breath, calculating just how much trouble I'm in. This could be the moment Dad kills me. I look down so I can at least remember the shirt I'm wearing when I die. It's orange and yellow and says *Love, Peace and Art* in a circle on the front. I kind of wish I had on the green one with the horseshoe on the back.

"Do you spend time at Mills? My mother-in-law plays cards there," Dad asks as he moves toward the desk.

My whole body cringes. The good news is the photo comment didn't process in his brain. The bad news is he thinks Naomi hangs out with Gram at the senior center.

She tilts her head in that I'm-now-totally-confused way.

I step forward. Confession at the ready.

Then I have an idea.

"Dad, Mr. Barker called. He said he's trying to open up the pharmacy and could use a hand shoveling. Asked if you'd come by."

Dad sighs and looks over at the boots he just took off.

"I can put the sand down in the front and back walkways of the B&B if you want to go and help Mr. Barker," I say.

"That's my girl." He looks over at Naomi and says, "Nice meeting you."

Before she can do anything but smile, he slides on his boots and heads out the door.

Naomi turns to me. "Your dad seems like a good man."

"He is," I say.

"Should I wait?" she asks.

I shake my head as I walk her to the door. "This kind of thing could take a while." As she leaves, I wonder if we'll hear back from Naomi. Not sure what to think of what just happened, but I'm thankful my secret's safe for one more day.

This snow day feels lucky. I find the last puzzle pieces we need to complete the mama beagle. Chocolate brown and black with a white belly and paws. Then I spread sand on the walkways, as promised, run upstairs, and take Winston out of his cage. He trolls up my arm and over my shoulders as I tell him about Naomi and ask him what he thinks is going to happen when Dad shows up at the pharmacy with his shovel. We both agree Mr. Barker will likely just be happy for the help. It's kind of what people do around here. Maybe that's why no one leaves.

Out the window, Lucy, Winston, and I stare at our foot-printless backyard. The B&B snow globe looks just like it does out my window. I call Elliot. In ten minutes, he's at my door in full snow gear, and we head outside. Lucy dives into the snow, nose first, looking for hidden anything, while Elliot and I make snow angels and our version of Frosty. This guy's got beet eyes, a parsnip nose, and cucumber slices for a mouth. Once our bodies are numb, we come inside for hot cocoa with cinnamon, marshmallows, and whipped cream.

"Next Thursday's the day," he says with a whipped cream mustache.

"Shh." I look around to make sure no one's around. "I don't live alone, you know."

He slurps the rest of his cocoa. "Got it." He slides closer and in a very quiet voice says, "I confirmed with my dad the date and time of the meeting. So we should be clear to go."

I pick the marshmallows from the bottom of my mug.

He guzzles the last of his cocoa and grabs his coat. "Come on. Let's go."

"Where?"

"To find Mickey Hogan."

"Dead Mickey Hogan?"

"Exactly."

31

The Gnomes

"Wait, I thought you thought he was dead and his ghost was flying around the B&B?" I ask, trailing behind Elliot through the snow.

"I do."

"So where are we going?"

"To his house."

I stop walking.

"I hate to ask the obvious, but why are we going to the house of a person who's dead and gone?"

"To find out what really happened?"

"Is this our trial break-in?" I ask.

He stops. "I hadn't thought of it that way."

"Did you think Dead Mickey was going to just let us in?"

He laughs and starts walking again. In five minutes, we're standing in front of a ranch-style brick house with white shutters. I can see the tops of two gnome statues sticking out of the snow, red cap next to green cap. They remind me of the one in Gram's room. I wonder if Mickey has lots of candles and tins and hangers. I start to brush the snow off green cap gnome to see what's under his cap, when I hear a creaking sound.

I slowly turn my head toward the noise as my brain frantically searches for the excuse I'm going to use for being at Dead Mickey's house. *We were just visiting. My aunt lives in the neighborhood. I'm selling Girl Scout cookies.* Then I see what's making the noise.

Elliot's opening the mailbox.

Creak. Creak. Creak.

I walk over and throw snow on his head. "You scared me!"

His eyebrows go scrunchy. "What are you talking about?"

"I heard the noise and thought someone was coming."

"Who cares if someone is coming? We're not doing anything wrong. We're just standing on the lawn. Anyway, take a look at this." He points to the inside of the mailbox. "It's packed." Then he pulls out a ton of mail.

I shove his hand back into the mailbox and look around. "Someone could see you. And I'm pretty sure it's a federal offense to take another person's mail."

"I'm not taking it. I'm just looking at it."

"Either way. Put it back."

"There's a lot in here. Look. Electric bill. Gas bill. Phone bill. All the envelopes have a big red stamp that says OVERDUE. A brochure to Aruba. Another one to Puerto Rico. And loads of magazines. *Real Estate Madness. Cooking Together. Guns, Bows, and Other Toys.*"

"Guns? And bows?"

Elliot puts the mail and magazines back into the mailbox. "Let's go," he says, walking toward the front door.

"I don't think this is such a good idea," I say as I follow him.

The front door is locked.

The side door is locked.

The back door is locked.

This is a sign. A go-home-right-now sign. "Okay, we tried, but this is a no go. Let's head back. I'm sure my dad could use some help clearing the rest of the snow." I tug on Elliot's coat, but he spins around and takes a step back.

"I bet it's here somewhere," he says, rubbing his hairless chin.

"What is?" I look around and see nothing but a potentially dead guy's abandoned house and lots of snow.

He walks over to a rock and lifts it up. "Look what I've got."

In his hand is a key.

32

Dead Mickey's Kitchen

I'm standing in the middle of Dead Mickey's kitchen. It's cold and smells like nothing. No cookies. No turkey dinner. No bacon. No muffins. Just nothing. It reminds me of my old house after Mom died. Not right after. Those first few days it was filled with gross food from lots of people I didn't know. Weeks after that, there was a whole lot of nothing but weepy sadness. And weepy sadness doesn't smell like anything.

"Hello!" Elliot shouts.

"Really? You think you can just break into someone's house and yell, 'Hello'? And when Dead Guy comes into the room with a shotgun, are you going to ask him about his day?"

"I would simply say that we knocked, that we're doing a survey on ghost sightings in the neighborhood, and that the door was open."

"And you think that would convince him *not* to shoot us?" I rub my arms to stop the chill from spreading through my body. It's not working. "What are we looking for anyway?"

Elliot walks into the den. "Clues. If Mickey's our ghost, maybe we can find something here to confirm it."

I walk into the kitchen. On the refrigerator is a teeth-cleaning reminder, a photo of a big, fat cat, and a calendar. One date three months ago is circled in black marker. I stare at the date, wondering if I'm supposed to know if it's a clue.

I decide I'm not and move on to the den.

Neither the worn, overstuffed brown recliner in the corner, the leather boots by the door, nor the stink of stale cigar smoke tell me anything. All I see are dead stuffed heads. Moose head. Deer head. Rabbit head. Squirrel heads—looks like a whole family.

Elliot moves down the hall into the bedroom. On the way, I try not to bump into the deer head staring at me with plastic eyes. I hear a loud bang coming from the backyard, and my neck stiffens. "We should go," I whisper.

"Soon." He peeks into the only room with a bed. "Look, it hasn't been slept in."

"Or maybe he makes his bed every morning." Like Mom used to do. I don't really remember, but Gram always tells me I don't have Mom's neat gene and then points to my unmade bed. She says I'm more like her.

He spins around to face me.

"Nope. No one's been here for a while. The mail hasn't been picked up. The dishes in the sink are crusty, the cigar smells old, and the boots look unworn—even though we've had snow."

Another loud clank comes from just outside. I ball my fists and squeeze my fears. I swallow hard when I ask this next question. "So where do you think he is?"

He stares back at me. "I don't know where exactly his body is, but I'd bet his ghost is at the B&B."

"Maybe we should call the police. I mean if Mickey really is dead and no longer going to wear his boots in the snow, we should tell someone. Do something."

"Not until we get more evidence. Right now, no one would believe us."

He's right. No one's going to believe a couple of kids with a ghost meter.

We walk out of the bedroom, down the hall, through the kitchen, out the back door, and around the house. Standing on the front lawn staring at us is a woman holding a snow shovel. She has a pointy chin, two long braids, and a wool hat with a large, brown pom-pom. "What are you kids doing here?" Her voice is sharp and accusing.

"We, um . . ." is all I get out before Elliot jumps in.

"We're conducting a ghost survey."

I can't believe he's going with ghost sightings.

"A what?" Braids steps closer. Too close, but I don't think this is the time to tell her that she's invading my personal space. I step back.

"I understand the confusion, ma'am. This is a new town service. There've been some complaints about ghosts in the area, so we're looking into it," Elliot says with the authority of someone who's actually telling the truth.

"We, as in you two kids?" she snaps, her voice louder.

Don't think this is working. We should have gone with Girl Scout cookies.

"Of course not," Elliot says. Clears throat. "The man heading up the initiative is Mr. Melville Jenkins, maybe you've heard of him. Mayor Hartman held a press conference last week recognizing the good work Jenkins has done for other towns with similar problems."

I can't believe it. She's nodding.

"Anyway," Elliot continues, "we're just volunteers conducting the survey."

"So what were you doing here at Mickey's?"

"We were just going to ask whoever lives here if he'd like to take the survey."

The angry etches on her face soften. "Haven't seen Mickey in months. Unlike him to disappear for so long."

I feel a sharp knot wedge into my stomach.

"He's got Mr. Cuddles to think about."

"Who's that?" I ask. My image of Dead Mickey doesn't fit with anything named Mr. Cuddles.

"His cat. Whenever he goes away, I take care of Mr. Cuddles. About three months ago, Mickey said he was going out of town. Asked me to look after Mr. Cuddles, and I haven't seen him since. He's usually never gone for more than a few days."

"Well, we hope your friend and his cat are fine. Would you like to take the survey?" Elliot asks.

"I don't believe in ghosts," Braids says as she trails back to her house.

I watch until I see her walk through her front door. "That was close." I exhale and try to breathe like a normal person for the first time since I spotted the gnomes. Then my phone pings.

It's a text from Jessica. **Sorry. Sorry. Meet me at library to rehearse. Sorry. Sorry.**

I text her back. **No.**

33

Dry Boots in the Snow

That night, all I can think about is Dead Mickey and his boots. Don't know why the boots stick in my head, but there they are, sitting in the kitchen. Dry. Abandoned. My mind traces back to what actually happened to Mickey.

I grab my purple butterfly book.

Dear Mom,

Not sure what to think about Mickey Hogan. Mostly I don't understand why no one is looking for him. I mean his neighbor Braids is worried, but she's not doing anything about it. Doesn't anyone care that he's missing?

That he doesn't have his boots and it's snowing? Doesn't he have people?

If I was gone, Gram would be worried that I didn't have my boots. I mean I think she would, even though now I'm not 100 percent sure since coral lipstick, perfume, and Mr. Sid Caldwell have come into the picture. Dad would be worried if it was lightning. 100 percent.

Does it snow in heaven? Do you need boots?

Just wondering.

Love you,
Francine

I roll over and read my letter to Winston. "Don't worry, if you were gone, I'd go looking for you. Lucy, too." Then I practice my rap to stop thinking about Dead Mickey. I must have fallen asleep somewhere between worrying about Mickey and rapping Shakespeare, because soon the sun is peeking through my shades and I smell Dad's waffles. I fly around the kitchen grabbing breakfast, my hat and gloves and scarf, and shove all of it into my backpack, while Dad's spouting a detailed list of instructions. Remember to put down more sand after school. Gone all day. Something about some meeting. I'm on my own for dinner. Stuff in fridge. Make the cookies. Love you.

I meet Elliot, breakfast in hand.

"You could be the best friend ever," he says as he stuffs the first waffle into his mouth.

I hand him a second waffle. "You mean, I *am* the best friend ever."

He nods.

When we get to the front of school, I see that Annie is surrounded by her flock of kindergarteners. She seems to be embracing her inner grape today. She's wearing a purple speckled hat, a purple-and-green-striped scarf that covers most of her face, and a matching winter coat. "Hello, friends!" she sings.

"Hello, friends," her flock echoes, followed by a bevy of giggles.

People would look for Annie if she went missing. I'd look for her.

Then she dips under her many layers, into her pocket, and pulls out a small bell. "I found this and thought of you. If you ever need anything, all you have to do is ring it."

"My own personal bat signal. I love it."

Her smile makes its way above the scarf line.

"The bell can be heard between the worlds of Lazos and home. If Fly and Fitzgerald were ever to get separated, all Fitzgerald would need to do would be to ring the bell and they could find their way back to each other."

I ring my bell. Nothing extraordinary happens. Except Elliot says I rang it too close to his ear and now he can't hear anything.

"Well, at least you won't be able to hear when Jessica tells you that you smell like beef jerky."

"Good point," he says as we walk into our classroom. That's when I realize today is the dress rehearsal for our presentations. And my costume is hanging over my desk chair.

At home.

I think about ringing my bell, flashing the bat signal, but I know neither will help.

Jessica is blanketed by her minions, and I'm not telling her that I'm not prepared in front of the vultures. I wonder who would start the search if she disappeared. Not the shadows by her side. Between the two of them, they couldn't find a single thing. Then I think about her mom crashed on the couch and her dad with his other family. Cracks in my mad wedge in.

Mr. Bearson runs through today's announcements. I catch the one about the float meeting and promptly erase it from my brain. Then he tells us he's extending the deadline for the float theme entries. "Reminder, I'm looking for everyone to participate."

He stares straight at me. I realize with everything happening, I still hadn't submitted a float idea. I search my brain, but the only thing I come up with is a float shaped like a giant waffle.

We break off into our pairs. I sit across from Jessica and dig into my backpack, trying to look like I'm searching for something important. Then I swallow hard, and say, "I left my costume at home."

I wait for the shriek and the indignant outrage, but it doesn't come. "Just bring it the day we present for real."

I look up to make sure a zombie hasn't taken over her body. It looks like Jessica, but I'm not totally convinced.

"I made these," she says, handing me posters of Lady Macbeth, the witches, and Macbeth.

"Wow! They're good." I try to hold on to the angry knot floating around my stomach, but feel it slowly slipping away.

For the rest of class, we rap Shakespeare. I realize between stanzas that if I don't submit a float idea soon, Mr. Bearson's going to call me up to his desk for a you're-not-in-trouble-but-this-is-still-embarrassing talk. Raheim and I are the only two who haven't pinned our ideas onto the board yet and I can see a very uncomfortable Raheim talking to Mr. Bearson now. I tell Jessica I need a rap break and quickly write the only thing spinning in my brain that doesn't have to do with waffles.

After we finish our run-through and I endure pre-algebra, the History of Civilization, and Spanish, I tack my idea to the Winter Family Festival Parade board.

And say a small thank-you to zebras everywhere.

34

Rule #11

"I'm moving out."

Gram's words trail up the stairs into my room and settle next to the rest of my worries behind my big toe.

"I don't want you to leave. No one wants you to leave, Bea. I just need you to remove your things from Yahtzee and the hall."

"I did."

"And then you found or bought or unfurled more stuff, which is back in the room and the hall."

"Need I remind you that space has been empty for months?" Gram says.

"That's not the point."

"What's not the point?" I ask, walking into the kitchen.

No one says anything.

"I mean it. I want to know. You both said everything was fine. That I shouldn't worry." I stare at their faces. "This isn't what fine looks like. Fine doesn't include Gram moving out."

"No one's moving out," Dad says.

"I wouldn't say that. I saw the dumpster," Gram says.

Dad paces between me and Gram. "We'll go through your things together."

"That's not happening," Gram says, unmoved by Dad's offer.

I look out the window and sitting behind the garbage bins is one large steel container. On the side in bright red block letters it says DANNY'S DUMPORIUM—ONE MAN'S TRASH IS ANOTHER MAN'S GOLD.

"Bea, we talked about this. Your stuff is a fire hazard."

"See, that's not fine," I say.

"I got a call from the health department yesterday. Someone complained," Dad continues. "I can't let them shut us down."

"My daughter would've never let you do this to me," Gram says.

"Do what? Take care of you?"

"Make me get rid of my things."

Dad's jaw twitches. "That's not fair."

"But it's true."

"I'm not—"

"Stop! Just stop." I step between them. "This isn't working and it's *not* fine." I grab my gold sparkle Sharpie from the treasure drawer (a gift from Mrs. Beasley the artist) and a piece of computer paper from the drawer and write out **Rule #11: No one's throwing anything out. No one's moving.** I tack the new rule to the wall and look at the two of them. "This is the new rule."

I walk outside. The falling snow mixes with the tears streaming down my cheeks.

Gram can't leave.

We need her here with us.

I need her here with me.

Even if I have to share her with Mr. Sid Caldwell.

I wipe the snow off the curb in front of Elliot's house and sit and breathe and cry. The worry and sadness that I stuffed behind my big toe twists inside me. I wait for the tears to stop, but they don't. They roll with purpose.

Then someone sits down next to me.

35

Maybe

"Are you okay?" Jessica asks me.

"Have you been following me?" I ask. I can smell the raspberry gum dancing around her mouth.

"No. You're the only loser who follows people around," she says. "This was my old house before Elliot moved here, remember?"

I don't answer. I don't want to hear her tell me to make Elliot take care of her blueberry bushes and roses. I don't want to remember living next door and being friends. All those memories are buried deep under her lies.

She stuffs another piece of gum in her mouth. "So are you okay?"

I nod as the tears slip down my cheeks.

"Not sure I believe you."

"You're not really the person I want to talk to right now."

She looks around. "No one else is here."

"I'm fine."

She laughs.

"What's so funny?"

"When we were eight and I told you the cookies you made were fine, you told me that you hated that word. That it meant nothing. Then you made me rank the cookies on a scale of one—the best thing I ever ate—to ten—going to puke."

A crack of a smile slips out. I remember. They were chocolate chip sugar cookies.

"So let's pretend I'm not the jerk who stole the jewelry and planted it in your pocket. Pretend I'm the friend you used to play hide-and-seek with in the B&B and almost won by hiding in the dryer. Until your gram turned it on."

The idea of pretending nestles around us.

"She says she's moving out," I say.

Screech. A car down the street skids on the ice.

"Who?"

I turn and look at my once friend. "Gram."

Jessica squeezes my hand like she used to when we watched scary movies. Just before I'd scream, run upstairs, and hide in my closet.

"She says everything's okay, but I know it's not."

"Remember the time we took her to get her first pair of cowboy boots."

I do. That day Jessica and I must have watched Gram try on twenty pairs of boots. They were all too tall. Too pointy. Too big. Too tight. Too not-just-right.

I laugh.

We sit like that for a while. Then I ask what's been on my mind since that day I followed her on the street. "What's your dad doing here? I thought he lived in Florida."

I hear her sigh and wish I hadn't said anything.

"He was in Florida. Then I got a call a few months ago after not hearing from him for over a year. He said he was back. With his family. His *new* family. And he wanted to spend time with me." She looks at me. "I wasn't ready to hang out with him and his new life, but I wanted to see him. So I did."

"Was that the day I saw you?"

"Followed me," she corrects.

"That was the first time you saw him since that day in fourth grade?"

She nods.

"Jessica, I'm sorry."

"Me too," she says, staring at the street. Then, "Can you call me Jess?"

"I guess, but why? You've been Jessica forever." Like when we made those T-shirts in third grade with our handprints and signed them *Frankie & Jessica*. And when we made friendship bracelets with letter beads at camp. Mine's sitting in my jewelry box. It says *Frankie and Jessica BFF.*

"My dad calls me Jessica."

Now I get it. We sit for a while saying nothing. Then Jess says, "I really am sorry about the other day. I know I messed up. I'm just trying to keep it together for Leila, with my mom being all . . ."

"All what?" I ask.

She's quiet for a minute, then says, "I guess tired and super sad all the time. She's been like this for a while now, but it's gotten worse since my dad moved back. She sleeps a lot and just, kind of, stopped doing all the mom stuff."

I don't even know what that is.

"So I've been trying to keep things normal. I thought if we celebrated my mom's birthday and ran the float stuff like we used to, maybe it would help. Maybe Leila would stop sneaking into my bed in the middle of the night and my mom would see that we're still a family. That my dad leaving hasn't changed that."

In that moment, I realize we're both trying to put our families back together.

Big, light snowflakes in no hurry to land fall gently around us, but neither of us gets up to leave. Then Jess breaks into our Macbeth rap. Around the second stanza, I join in.

When we finish, a speck of happiness finds its way into my heart.

A layer of snow coats my boots. "I've got to get back to make the cookies for the new guests." I don't say that I hope they haven't canceled.

"Yeah. I've got to get home, too."

When I walk into the B&B, neither Dad nor Gram is in the welcome area. But tacked to the wall is **Rule #11**. And, at the bottom of the page, I see both of their signatures.

I add a noseless smiley face.

36

Two Is a Pair of Socks

I've got just enough time to make sugar cookies with a sprinkle of nutmeg. I leave out the chocolate chips. I remember Jess only gave that recipe a four—would eat them again if they were the only dessert. I still don't see Dad anywhere, but then I remember he said something about being out late. Now that I think about it, he's been gone a lot lately. I can't recall where he said he'd be. Nothing surfaces, so I take the cookies out of the oven and check the messages at the desk. There's one from Naomi. *Uh-oh.* The profile lists my cell. Never thought the Possibles would call Dad at the B&B. If one of them actually reaches him, I'm dead. Or grounded for life. Both equally possible.

I quickly run upstairs and write Naomi an email from Dad.

Sorry our meeting was so short. You seem very nice, but I think we'd be better as friends.

I call Elliot. "Does that sound okay? I don't want to hurt her feelings. She's nice. She's just Mabel nice." Lucy noses open my door, grabs my right boot, and jumps onto my bed.

"Well, keep out the part where you tell her she's old."

I add another line about how glad I was to meet her. This last part is more about me. Then I read Elliot a new message from the latest Possible.

You sound great. I love B&Bs and pets, and your daughter seems wonderful, too. I am currently in Beijing working on a cryogenics research project, but will be thawed and back in the States in seven months. Would love to connect.

Signed,
Wait for me?

"Is she kidding?" I ask Elliot.

"I hope so."

"Brad" responds with a thoughtful and polite *nope*. Then I slide her name into the Impossibles column right next to Georgia, Naomi, and Evelyn. As I hang up with Elliot, I wonder if I'll ever find a Possible and be part of a family again.

Dear Mom,

Do you think my plan is going to work? Please don't be mad. I just want to be a family again. Like before. The three of us. Not just Dad and me. Not two. Two is a pair of socks, yin and yang, war and peace. Two is sandwich bread. Our family was never two slices. Our family never fit on a bicycle. I just want what we had. I want our pieces back.

Besides, if I can find a mom, then maybe Dad won't be so focused on Gram. And she won't move out. Not ever.

But if I'm being spill-the-beans honest, I'm kind of nervous. What if Dad doesn't want this? What if he wants to fit on a bicycle? What if I'm making a mistake? A. Big. Fat. Mistake.

Love you,
Francine

My phone rings. It's Elliot.

"Didn't we just hang up?"

"The timetable has changed." His voice sounds like a fifty-year-old newsman is broadcasting live from inside his body.

"What are you talking about?"

"My dad's meeting—the one Reggie is supposed to go to—has been rescheduled. Something about an upcoming snowstorm."

"Sometimes I hate winter." I rub Lucy's belly as she stretches out across my comforter. "So when's our break-in scheduled for now?"

"Tomorrow."

37

Gatekeeper and the Cookies

At the float meeting that Elliot made me go to the next day, I spin the plastic four-leaf-clover in my pocket. It's the one Annie gave me. She said it was for Fitzgerald. That everyone needed extra luck. I'm a fan. Of Annie and luck. I also made a wish when the clock hit 11:11. I consider both very good signs for my day not ending in prison. But time drags and the flips in my stomach show no sign of slowing down. I can't even think about eating the tacos Shanti's mom donated to the after-school float meeting. No chicken taco with cilantro, hot sauce, beans, guacamole, and extra cheese. I eat a package of dry crackers and hope I don't puke all over my lap.

"Let's go to the library after the meeting to work on our rap," Jess says. It's not really a suggestion, more like a that's-what-we're-doing.

"Can't." Figure I'll leave out the details—that I'll be spending the afternoon breaking into Reggie's office with a box of cookies and a bad excuse to find out what's going on with Dead Mickey and the B&B.

"Our presentation is next week. Could even be Tuesday if Charlie and Ashley finish early."

"I'm aware of our upcoming rap debut. Just can't practice later today."

"Doctor's appointment?"

"Nope."

"Dentist?"

"Nope."

"Gram?"

"Just can't." No need to bring Gram into this. "Have to help my dad with some stuff."

Which is not entirely false.

"Fine." She smiles.

After the float meeting, I reconnect with Elliot in Headquarters with a box of cookies.

"You're late," I say as I hand him the cookies. "I thought you were just stopping home to grab the map?"

"Sorry. Ran into my mom who promptly gave me a new nonemergency emergency to-do list. I even negotiated an early release, but I had to promise to be home by five thirty to finish." He opens the lid to the cookie box.

"Don't eat those. We need them. They're my cover."

"I know. I just want to smell them. I mean this one here, this chocolate thing, smells so good."

I close the lid before smelling turns to tasting turns to one missing. "What was the nonemergency emergency this time?"

"The spices needed to be organized alphabetically."

I think of all the spices at the B&B and try to imagine how long it would take to put them in alphabetical order.

"I was almost done, until I found the smoked paprika. Then I had to go in and reshuffle because it didn't fit."

"Did you put it under *S* or *P*?"

"*S*."

"Hmm."

"Why 'hmm'? It starts with an *S*."

"But it's paprika, so I'd put it under *P*. The way a library or bookstore ignores the word 'the' when they alphabetize books."

"I never got why they do that. I mean, it's in the title," Elliot says, pulling the map of Reggie's office building out of his backpack. "Remember, if anyone asks, you're just there to deliver cookies."

"And that's not weird or obvious?" Seems to scream weird *and* obvious to me.

He stares at the plans.

"Were you like some sort of spy in a former life?" I'm almost convinced that could be true.

"Hope so," he says.

"Remind me again why I'm the one going in and you're the one sitting in the lobby?"

"Because I have no reason at all for being in Reggie's office. Just showing up would raise suspicion. But you do. He's been hounding your dad."

"So that makes me showing up with a box of cookies from the B&B not weird?"

"Not *that* weird. It's like when my family moved next door and your gram brought over her famous chocolate, chocolate cookies. The cookies are like a normal neighborly gesture."

"Nothing about this fits any definition of normal," I say.

"It's normal enough."

"I'll be waiting here." He points to an area on the map. "And I'll have my phone, so I'll be with you the whole time."

"Except you won't be breaking the law with baked goods."

"Look, if you go to jail, we both go to jail."

"Feeling better already."

We walk the six blocks through the snow to Reggie's office. The building is skinny and taller than most with a lobby that's too bright. Elliot settles onto a leather bench. A woman in a pencil skirt, blazer, and silk shirt passes us.

She's barking into her phone and walking like her spiky blue heels are on fire.

"You really needed to bring that?" I point to the ghost-hunting laser in Elliot's hand.

"I'm blending in," he says.

If I wasn't so nervous, I'd burst out laughing.

"You've got this," he says.

"Easy for you to say while sitting on the bench with your laser in the lobby."

I take my four-leaf clover, the cookies, and what's left of my confidence, and make my way to the elevators, where I bump into a woman with a crying baby in a stroller and a man in a suit with a scowl. Don't faint, I tell myself as I take a deep breath. A brief moment of happiness fills me when I realize there's no thirteenth floor. Then I hit the button for the fifteenth floor, and wedge myself between someone who desperately needs to go home early to shower and someone who had an Italian sub for lunch. Lean toward Sub Man and try to ignore the nausea swirling around my belly.

The doors open, and I follow the signs left and right and then left again. The tan swirls on the carpet make me dizzy. Definitely don't need another reason to puke, so I steady myself as I open the door to the outer office of the real estate company and get ready to make my move.

Sitting at a large desk in front of the hall is a woman with a bun, a long neck, and a fire engine red face—the gatekeeper of all-things Reggie.

"May I help you?" Gatekeeper asks.

"I have cookies for Mr. Hogan." The lie slides out easier than expected.

"Well, Mr. Hogan isn't here right now."

"If it's okay, I could just put them on his desk and leave them as a surprise for when he returns," I suggest, as if surprising Reggie is something I might actually do.

Smile big.

Act normal.

Breathe.

"You can leave them with me, or wait for him to return. But you can't go into his office until he gets back."

I eye Gatekeeper. She doesn't seem like the kind of woman who's going to change her mind. "I'll wait." I figure this will give Elliot and me time to revise our plan.

I text Elliot to devise a new strategy and find a plan B.

I have no signal.

No service.

No Elliot.

38

Waiting for a Sign

So much for being with me the whole time.

The air in the waiting room feels stiff like stale bread. I look around and realize I need a plan. Sitting here is *not* a plan.

Think.

Think.

Think.

The cookies and I get up. "Excuse me," I ask politely. "Is there a bathroom I can use?"

Gatekeeper glares at me suspiciously, unless that's just her natural face. Which seems totally possible. "Down the hall, then right, second left, and first right. It'll be on your left," she tells me.

The first hall is mint green. Not sure why that's a good choice. I weave to my right and left staring at every door in the pastel-colored halls. Thomas Jameson. Cecily Richards. Matthew Sterling. Juan Garcia. Brianna Jackson. I hope I can find my way back. Next right. Patrice Kendrick. Second door down, across from the bathroom, I see a sign for Reggie Hogan.

The cookies rattle in the box. *Just be normal*, I tell myself. But it's not working.

Normal is nowhere.

I look down the hall, and when I don't see anyone coming, I knock on the door.

No answer.

Take a deep breath, turn the knob, and step inside.

The office smells like burger grease. Like Reggie. On the walls, there are pictures of Reggie holding a big fish, Reggie in the woods, Reggie and some guy who looks like Reggie, and one of an old man with a long gray beard. I set the cookies on his desk next to a mug filled with toothpicks, and take out my phone. Still no service, but at least the battery isn't dead. I snap pictures of the papers and stuff scattered on top of Reggie's desk. Not exactly sure what I'm looking for, but Elliot said to document everything, you never know where the clues are hiding. Secretly I wish this were a board game that came with directions: *Go three spaces, select a card, read the clue, and find the evidence you need to solve the mystery.* My hands shake. Steady and *click*. And *click*. And *click*. Don't bother looking at the pictures now. Mostly just praying my hangnail doesn't bleed on anything.

Then I move to the desk. The top right drawer is locked. So is the one on the bottom right. But when I pull on the bottom left drawer, it opens. There are piles of papers and folders stuffed inside. Look at my watch. Running out of time. The room snatches my breath. Stealing my nerve.

Focus. Help Dad, I tell myself as I continue the hunt.

Snap. I take pictures of Reggie's chair. His toothpicks. Each file, hoping these will tell us something. Anything.

As I pick up the last folder, I notice the address across the tab. 51 Lincoln Street, Dennisville, Vermont.

That's the B&B.

My home.

My fingers shake as I open the file. There are architectural plans and letters from the bank and emails. Lots of emails. Then a photo slips out.

The yellow dress startles me.

I hear footsteps in the hall and quickly slip the photo back into the file and close the drawer.

But I can't leave her here. My brain spins while my hands take over, opening the drawer, taking the photo, and stuffing it in my pocket.

I close the drawer a little harder than I mean to, slowly back out of the office, and walk quickly but not too quickly down the hall.

"Good afternoon," a man in a paisley tie says. By the time I catch my breath to say anything, the guy's around the corner.

In the bathroom, I splash water on my face and try to breathe normally, but I'm not sure it's working. I stare at myself in the mirror. My mind spins, trying hard to justify what I just did. Dad needs me. I'm his person. I wait for a sign telling me that it's all okay. The lights to flash. The hot water to turn on. The toilet to suddenly flush. But none of that happens.

So I weave my way back to the waiting room, trying to remember if it's Creamsicle to new snow to something else to mint green. I'm almost there. But just as I turn the corner to the last hall, *smack!*

I run right into Reggie Hogan.

39

Where Are They?

"What are *you* doing here?" Reggie wants to know.

Helping my dad. I don't say that. Actually, I don't say anything. The air in my lungs deflates and my brain shuts down.

"I asked you a question, little lady? What are you doing wandering the halls of my office?"

"Bathroom."

He pulls the gnawed-on toothpick out of his mouth. "Doesn't that B&B of yours have plumbing?"

I nod. "I meant I needed the bathroom while I waited for you."

"Why in blazing glory did you come to see me?"

"Cookies."

201

He looks around.

"I brought cookies. From my dad. For not being able to meet."

"Well, I'll be."

"They're still warm. I mean, they were when I got here."

"Great. I'm starving." He rubs his too-many-burgers belly. "Those zoning and permit meetings are nothing but a bunch of poorly dressed men and women serving up bologna sandwiches with mayonnaise. Let's have at those cookies."

I freeze.

My hands are empty. *Where are the cookies?* My mind rewinds. The bathroom. The man in the hall. The office. I stop breathing. The cookies are on the desk in the office. Reggie's office. *Think. Think. Think.*

"I put them on your desk."

"My desk?"

I nod again.

"Who let you into my office?" Growl.

"Um, the door was open." Not exactly, but it wasn't locked. "I was going to the bathroom and realized it was getting late and that I'd have to leave the cookies with, um, that lady at the front desk." Pause. "And, well, I wasn't sure that was such a good idea, so when I saw that your office door was open, I just put them in there." I hold my breath. *Please, please, please believe me.*

He snorts and laughs, and I exhale.

"That Ms. Limestone's a good woman, but she has been known to consume a dozen cookies in one sitting."

I love Gatekeeper.

He moves toward his office and my heart freezes. I feel Mom's photo in my pocket. Can't go in there. I look at my watch. "I've got to get back to the B&B," I say, as if that's the only reason I need to leave this place immediately. "Enjoy the cookies."

"Well, you be sure to tell your daddy that while I appreciate these here cookies, which I do, he's running out of time."

As I speed-walk down the mint-green hall, past Gatekeeper, and into the elevators, Reggie's words bounce around my brain. Running out of time for what?

The bright white lobby reminds me of disinfectant. A woman with a briefcase and tappy heels trots past me. A bald man's yelling into his phone. And Elliot's still sitting where I left him, worry carved across his face.

"What happened? It's been twenty-eight minutes since you left. This was supposed to take thirteen total. Why didn't you call?"

The yelling man stomps his shiny loafers and swears something Gram would not be happy about.

"There's no service up there."

Elliot's face turns that weird shade of green it turned the day I took him on the upside-down roller coaster at Peak

Park. "Oh," he says, and then falls silent as we walk out the door.

Back at Headquarters with the cardboard door closed, I tell him what happened.

"You all right?" he asks in a voice that sounds like it's covered in the blanket I wrap around myself during lightning storms.

"Yeah." I try to sound braver than I am.

"Sorry, Frankie," Elliot says, and I know he means it. "We're okay, right?" Something Elliot always needs to know.

I nod.

His complexion's coming back to a less alien color. "Let's see what you got."

We scroll through the photos on my phone.

Boring. Boring. Boring.

I bite my right pinkie nail as I decide whether to tell Elliot about the picture I stole.

"Maybe we're wrong," I say. "As much as I don't like Reggie, maybe he's got nothing to do with the ghost."

"Maybe," Elliot says as he zooms in on each picture for a closer look.

"There's something else."

He looks up.

"I found a photo in his files. Of my mom."

"Your mom?" he asks. "You sure?"

"Yep."

"Weird."

I agree because it *is* weird. Hugely weird. I knew they both grew up here, but there's no way the guy who doesn't give out Halloween candy was friends with my mom. No way.

Then Elliot stops scrolling. "Take a look at these three photos."

They're of plans to build some big thing. "So?"

"Frankie, Reggie wants to develop this area. Build condos or apartments or something. That's why he's been talking to your dad."

"What does my dad have to do with it?"

"Because it looks like he wants to build on the land where your B&B is."

"How do you know?"

"I don't. Not for sure. I have to finish going through all this stuff," he says. "But look at the surrounding area. That's Maisy's Florist, Sal's General Store, and Bert's Ice Cream Shack. And the land where he wants to build a big development he calls Hogan West looks like it's sitting right where the B&B should be."

"But we're here. It's not like he can build on top of us."

"He can if he owns the land."

"But he doesn't. And my dad said he'd never sell."

Elliot scratches his chin. "That's the part I don't get." Then his eyes roll into the back of his head.

"And what does the dead guy have to do with all of this?" I ask, wondering if the ghost can hear me.

"Don't know yet. I need time to connect the pieces," Elliot says. "But I can't do it now. I promised my mom I'd be back by five thirty to finish her nonemergency emergency to-dos."

When Elliot leaves, I take out the photo of my mom in the yellow dress. I didn't give this one to Elliot. This mystery is mine. I look at her smile and realize it reaches all the way up to her eyes.

Dear Mom,

I gotta know. What were you doing in Reggie's desk? Tell me.

Okay, I get it. I'll wait, but you should know that while you're hanging out in the cemetery looking after little Nate with Gertrude, Markus, and Beverly, I'm here, trying to fix things.

And if I'm being only-you-can-hear-me honest, I'm scared. Like lightning scared. Scared to find out what's going on. It's like the part in The Wizard of Oz when Dorothy pulls back the curtain and sees the great and powerful Oz. You know I always hated that part. Not sure I really want to know what's behind the curtain. But if I don't find out, who will help Dad? You're gone and Gram's with Sid.

I'm his person now.

Love you,
Francine

40

Mr. So and So

I shove the flies swarming around my stomach into the spot behind my big toe. Today's the day. Shakespeare Rap Day. I stand in front of my mirror, take a deep start-over breath, and practice the lyrics. My costume's packed and ready to go. Dad meets me downstairs with my favorite breakfast— gooey fried eggs, sausage, and ketchup on an English muffin.

"Good luck today," he says, sipping his coffee. "I'm really proud of you."

"Thanks, Dad." The breakfast room is quiet. I don't ask Dad where everybody is because I don't want him to tell me Mr. So and So and Mrs. This and That canceled because of rain or snow or a pulled back or an infected toenail, because I won't believe him anyway. And the look in his eyes that he's trying to hide from me tells me that he doesn't believe it, either.

"I have a meeting at the bank, but I'll be home for dinner together."

"Sounds like a plan."

Elliot's waiting for me at the end of the driveway. I hand him an English muffin. "Love when you have a big day," he says, biting into the breakfast sandwich.

On the way to school, he tells me he's sifted through 50 percent of the photos I took, but his mom had him cleaning out the garage most of yesterday. So we leave unsaid all the pickles in the path to figuring out what Reggie's up to, and Elliot gives me a beat so I can practice my rap. "It's really good," he says as he pops the last bite of sandwich into his mouth.

When we get to the front of the school, there's an old, round man in a crumpled, blue button-down surrounded by a swarm of five-year-olds. "Where's Annie?" I ask Blue Shirt.

"Don't know. Just got a call because the school needed a kindergarten sub."

I dig into my brain to try and remember Annie ever missing a day, but I can't. She was here my first day at Dennisville Elementary. I'd just moved, and my nerves had nowhere to hide. As I scoured the corner of the kindergarten room with the tubs of wooden blocks looking for a friend, she handed me a shiny plastic mouse. I loved him, named him Fly, and kept him in my pocket for the entire first month of school. Now he sits on my windowsill above my desk and Annie and I make up stories about the parallel universe he travels to when I'm not around. "Did they say she was sick? On vacation?"

"They didn't say anything, except when and where I needed to be. Sorry, kid."

My worry meter ticks. I spin the four-leaf clover Annie gave me and hope she's okay. She probably just has a cold or something.

Jess grabs me as soon as I step into Mr. Bearson's classroom.

"Did you remember the costume?"

"Yep."

"Practice?"

"Yep."

"Still mad?"

No answer. If I'm being totally honest, my mad seeped out the day she caught me crying in front of the B&B.

Sophie and Josh present first. They created an interactive Shakespeare museum. When they finish, they hand out free coupons to visit their museum. I clap and woot. I'd totally go to that museum.

Next up is Shanti and Jake. They act out the balcony scene from *Romeo and Juliet*. When they're finished, they take a bow.

"Okay, Jessica and Frankie. You're up," Mr. Bearson says as he straightens his Snoopy and Charlie Brown tie.

The rap's playing on a loop in my head. It's been doing that since I woke up this morning. I'm ready. I can do this. I look at Jess. She looks less ready or maybe more nervous.

I have an idea.

I don't ask Jess or Mr. Bearson, I just go with it. Trust your gut. Isn't that what Gram's always telling me?

I grab Elliot and whisper something in his ear. Jess seems annoyed or confused, though I can't really tell which. They look the same on her.

Then Elliot gives us a beat, and Jess nods and smiles. We set our posters on the lip of the whiteboard behind us as the class joins in the music. Greg taps his boot, Shanti drums her pencil, and Josh clacks his highlighters—one in each hand. Then we break into our Shakespeare rap. In that moment, I'm more convinced than ever that Reggie is like a modern-day Macbeth, all about greed and power.

When we're done, we're breathless, and our classmates stand and clap and cheer. A happy dance zips through my body.

41

Red Polish, Silver Glitter, and Pink Roses

After school, I burst through the door of the B&B to tell Dad about the rap. Once I fly upstairs, toss my backpack on the bed with Lucy, and give her some lovin', I peak into the Checkers Room to see if Dad's fixing the radiator again. But he's nowhere.

Then I remember. Out late. Bank thingy. Let's have dinner.

I knock on Gram's bedroom door so I can tell her about my triumphant performance. No answer. She's not home, but thankfully her stuff is not overflowing into Yahtzee or spilling into the hallway. **Rule #11** seems to be working. I lean against Gram's door and take out the photo of Mom in the yellow dress that I now carry with me.

Part of me wishes I remembered more about her.

All of me wishes I didn't have to.

Before I head to the senior center, I dip into the Trinket Treasure drawer, pull out a mood ring, and slip it on my ring finger. The rap begins to replay in my head and the ring turns happy purple.

When I get to Mills, Gram's in the card room. She's wearing her now signature coral lipstick and holding hands with Mr. Caldwell. I realize they're a package deal. Kind of like Dad and me.

I tell them about the rap. They want to hear it, and I think about belting it out right there in the middle of the room, but then I get an idea.

I text Jess.

Within an hour, she meets me in the card room. She looks confused as she walks over to our table and hugs Sid. "Pop! I didn't know you'd be here today."

"Pop?" I ask.

"This is my grandfather," Jess says.

"Today is so weird," is all I can say.

After we get over the fact that my gram and her pop are dating, we gather all the seniors into the center of the room and move sleeping Phil to the side. MaryKate from the front desk nods and gives us a beat. Jess and I move to the front of the room and perform our Macbeth rap. When we finish, everyone in the room is clapping.

Afterward, Gram and I talk and play cards for a while. I lose three games and am losing a fourth. "Why bright red?" I ask as she takes an ace of clubs from the pile.

She spreads her candy apple red nails out on the table and nods to the table where Jess and Sid are visiting. "It's his favorite." She moves around the cards in her hand. "What do you think of it?"

"I, um, like it." It's going to take a while to get used to the polish, the lipstick, the perfume. And Sid.

I'm about to ask her why Reggie would have a photo of Mom when there's a knock on the door and MaryKate walks in, holding a box filled with art supplies. I know because I have one of those boxes in Dad's office on the second shelf from the bottom. You never know when you're going to need glitter.

"Who wants to make Valentine's cards," asks MaryKate. With Dead Mickey, the quiet B&B, Operation Mom, and Reggie, I totally forgot that tomorrow is Valentine's Day.

Gram looks at me and winks. Or maybe she's looking past me at Sid, who's definitely looking at her. Jess, Sid, Gram, Mabel, Mae, Gerry, Shelby, and I spend the next hour making cards. By the end, there are about twenty red hearts full of glitter and stickers and strands of feathers spread across the table. I look over at Gram. She's covered in red and silver glitter. She and Sid fall onto the puffy couch, look at each other, and laugh.

Most of me is happy for her.

When I get back to the B&B, there are pink roses on the doorstep. I smile and am so thankful for my dad. He remembered. Every year, he gives me roses the night before so I wake up to them on Valentine's Day. Usually, they're yellow.

I pick up the vase and read the card—FOR: BRAD GREENE. They're not *from* Dad—they're *for* Dad.

42

Used Up All My Wishes

Who sent these? Dad's not with anyone. That's the whole point of Operation Mom. But if I didn't send them and Gram didn't send them, who did?

Then it hits me. He's been gone a lot. I thought he was at the bank or getting supplies at Harry's Hardware or helping the neighbors or doing dad stuff.

I should be happy. Thrilled. He's dating and the opposite of boring and he's not alone. We can go to the parade as a family. I have what's been missing. This is what I've wanted.

The pink flowers and I go inside the B&B. Lucy sprints up to me, baying and licking like it's been forever since I left. I hug her and tell her Dad's secret. She's unimpressed, grabs a pair of stray socks that must have fallen out of the laundry basket on the way to the washing machine, and runs upstairs. I head to the kitchen and plunk down on a stool at the counter, spinning 'round and 'round and 'round.

Be happy, I tell myself. *Gram's happy. Dad's happy. You should be happy, too.*

My mood ring turns gray.

I grab my computer and read Dad's profile. Obviously he doesn't need *my* help. A twinge of sadness creeps into my heart. I thought he needed me. I thought I was his person.

There are only twenty-four days until the parade.

He doesn't need me.

The mood ring's gray morphs to a murky black.

Dad walks into the kitchen holding a bouquet of yellow roses. "Happy Valentine's Day," he says.

I run up to my room and close the door. Then I grab my butterfly book and write as fast as my heart is beating. Dad knocks, but I don't answer. Not yet. I need to do this first.

Dear Mom,

Don't know what's wrong with me. I wanted Dad to find me a mom. No offense, just one that's alive. I wanted to be a family of three again. I even used up all my wishes on it—the one I made on the first star I saw every night, when the clock said 11:11, every time I found an eyelash on my cheek, when I closed my eyes just before I fell asleep. I always wished for the same thing. But now pink roses are here and it feels like a big bag of mixed-up puzzle pieces.

What do I do? What would you do?

I wish you were here right now.

Love you,

Francine.

Knock. Knock.

I can't ignore him again. I know he'll just keep coming back. I stuff my butterfly book under my mattress and say, "Come in."

The door opens, and Dad pokes his head in. His hair is still wet from the snow, his boots are off. Socks on. No holes. He puts the vase with my yellow roses on my desk, right next to a photo of me and Gram and Dad apple picking two years ago. Gram made the best apple crisp that night.

"Hey," he says, scooting next to me on the floor. My blue shag carpet's like an ocean between us. "You okay?"

I nod.

"I rarely get that reaction when I give someone flowers."

An unwanted smile sneaks out.

Dad continues. "But then I saw the pink ones, and I got it."

I don't say anything.

"I should've told you but wanted to wait," he says.

"Until what?" I pull off the plaid duct tape, pick at my hangnail, and wait for his answer.

He shrugs. "Not sure. I guess I thought as time went on, I'd know what to say. But now it's here and I don't." He brushes straggles of hair out of my eyes, and we sit like this for a while.

"How long have you been dating her?"

"About six months."

Six months! All that time I thought he was alone. Lonely.

"Does Gram know?"

His eyes smile and he nods. "That woman knows everything." We both laugh. "I'm sorry you found out like this. I should've been honest from the start."

He's not the only one keeping secrets. I grab my laptop and open it.

He stares at his profile. His photo. As he clicks and reads, his eyes widen, but he says nothing. The quiet is so loud I want to hide. Or scream. Or both.

"You shouldn't have."

"I was just trying to help."

"By soliciting me on the open market?"

"I never really thought about it like that. Maybe that should be a new rule, **Number Twelve: No soliciting.**"

He doesn't laugh.

"I didn't want you to be alone. Or sad. Or lonely. And—" The words stick in the very back of my throat.

"What?"

"I wanted to go to the Winter Family Festival parade as, well, a family."

He looks me straight in my eyes so nothing can slip out. "We *are* a family, Francine. We don't need another person to make us one." He holds my hands. I can feel the callus on his right palm.

A tear quietly drops off my cheek. Dad wipes it away like he did when I was little, and I hug him tight. We stay on my blue ocean for a while talking about my Shakespeare rap and the Valentine's art fest with Gram.

Then I dig deep to the place where I keep my lightning brave, and ask, "Do I get to meet Pink Roses?"

"You already have."

My brain runs through at roller-coaster speed any single woman who's been near my dad or the B&B for the last six months. Georgia. Evelyn. Naomi. Mabel (she stopped by to get something from Gram last Saturday). Grocery Delivery Lady. Cheese Delivery Lady.

"Who is she?"

He takes a big breath in. "Annie."

"Annie, my kindergarten teacher?"

He nods.

"Annie, Mom's friend?"

"That's the one."

43

A Long Minute of Nothing

Like eating a big plate of spaghetti and meatballs, it takes a long time to digest what Dad told me. Over the next few days, I try to understand it, forget it, put it behind my big toe. But none of that seems to be working. I sit on my bed and tell tail-chasing Lucy and burrowing Winston about Pink Roses. Then I wonder how many people a person gets.

When I can't convince myself it's more than one, I grab my list of potential mom questions to see how many I can answer about Annie.

1. Do you want a kid? An eleven-year-old girl to be specific?

Definite maybe.

2. Do you like pets? A beagle and an African pygmy hedgehog?

I know she has a parrot named Taco.

3. Do you want to live in Dennisville, Vermont?

Already does. That one was easy.

4. Do you want to live in a bed-and-breakfast?

No idea.

5. Can you bake?

I know she can't. One time, she brought brownies to school. Elliot and I ended up tossing ours in the bathroom trash. They were somewhere between disgusting and inedible.

6. Do you know how to draw a unicorn horn?

Don't know.

7. Do you like to hike? Ride bikes? Rock climb?

I've seen her riding her mountain bike around town.

8. Do you like the rain?

No idea.

9. Are you afraid of lightning?

No clue.

10. What's your favorite game?

This one's easy. I know it's Scrabble. Just like Mom. Just like my room. Just like me.

11. Do you like puzzles?

Don't know.

12. Are you free the day of the Winter Family Festival Parade?

I know the answer is yes, because every year she makes hot cocoa and hands it out to all the parade goers.

13. Are you handy?

No idea.

14. Would you feed Lucy and Winston if I were ever gone?

Not sure, but if she's feeding Taco, can't see why she couldn't feed Lucy and Winston, too.

15. Do you like me?

Yes. I mean she seems to, unless she's just being nice because she was Mom's friend and Mom died.

Fifteen questions. Six positive point scores. One negative. Three maybes. And five I can't answer. I hoped the list would make me feel less weird about this whole thing. But it doesn't.

I hop off my bed, grab my sketch pad and colored pencils, quietly slide out the front door, and text Dad an I-won't-be-gone-long message.

When I land at Weinstein's Cemetery, I lean my bike against the wire fence, and settle in next to Mom. The quiet wraps around us like Mrs. Rudabaker's afghan. "So all this stuff is happening that you need to know," I tell her. "Gram's seeing Sid Caldwell, who happens to be Jess's grandpa. And she seems happy, but it's kind of weird because now she always smells like flowers and wears lipstick."

I close my eyes for a second and get ready to share the other gigantic news. "Also, Dad's dating Annie. You heard me right. Annie. Your best friend." As I say it out loud, my mind feels twisty and my heart feels heavy like my backpack when I have homework in every subject. I don't know what to do with this feeling. It won't fit behind my big toe.

I pause for no reason other than my voice feels stuck. When it unsticks, I say, "I wish you were here. Then we'd still live in our red brick house in Boston, and Annie would just be *your* friend and Gram would just be Gram."

I say nothing for a while, hoping I can swallow my heap of sadness. But I can't. It leaks out, one salty teardrop after another.

Then I take in a huge breath of dead-people-live-here air and ask my mom, "If you have all your cemetery people, Dad has Annie, and Gram has Sid, who do I have? Who's my person?"

Not sure what I think will happen when I ask the question. I guess I hope that maybe Mom will answer me or give me some kind of everything-will-be-okay sign. But nothing happens. And for a long minute, the cemetery is totally still.

Then a small boy wearing a dinosaur shirt and holding his mom's hand, sits down next to Gertrude. They leave her daffodils and the boy tells his grandma Gertie that he won his soccer match. She doesn't respond.

A sadness I understand creeps across his tiny brow. I hand him a piece of paper, and together we color pictures for those who can't answer.

44

All of My Secrets

On the way home, I make one stop. My hand shakes a little as I ring the doorbell and stand still, nervously counting inside. The last time I showed up unannounced it wasn't exactly a welcomed surprise. I see a neighbor going into his apartment with a cup of coffee. He nods. I wave. I ring the doorbell again. The door's still closed.

Finally, it opens. Jess stands there. I wait to see if she's mad that I'm here—the place where her secrets are hidden, but she waves me in. No sign of mad. I step in. And suddenly I'm not sure why I'm here.

Leila runs up and hugs me. As she wraps her little arms around my neck, she asks, "Are you staying for dinner?"

I look at Jess. She hands me a cookie sheet. "You two can make dessert." I text Dad the new plan. Leila's curls bounce as she hops up and down. I glance at the couch to the right and am relieved not to see their mom sleeping. Jess puts on music, and the three of us dance around the kitchen like friends who don't keep secrets. When Leila ditches cooking for Legos, I tell Jess everything about Pink Roses, Operation Mom, and Reggie. And that's when I realize why I'm here. I'm sick of hiding and half-truths and friends-turned-not-turned-something-else.

"Wow! Impressive."

I stare at her. "Soliciting my dad and breaking and entering? I think you may need to rethink your definition of impressive."

"No. Doing all that for your dad. I mean, to make sure he's okay."

In that moment, I know we're the same. She did the things she did for her mom, and I did what I had to for my dad. We sit on the wood floor and watch Leila build a blue and yellow and red castle.

Then Jess disappears into her room. When she returns, she's wearing her *Jessica and Frankie BFF* bracelet. She slides next to me on the floor and says, "I went to see him."

"Who?" I ask, putting the cookies into the oven.

"My dad."

I look into her eyes to see if she's lying or sad. She isn't.

"I mean, I went to see him on purpose. No hiding behind a bush."

"How was it?" I ask.

"Weird. But okay, I guess."

Somewhere between the fried chicken, mashed potatoes, and double chocolate chip cookies, Jess's mom walks in the front door. I wonder if the vibe will shift. But it doesn't. Mrs. Blaine looks like the mom I remember. The one who helped us run a bake sale in third grade to raise money for the local fire station. She's wearing regular mom clothes and asks me mom questions. How's school? How's the float? How's your dad? And she joins us for dinner, in a chair at the table.

"Sorry you had to see me like that the other day," she says to me as she buries her embarrassment in the heap of potatoes on her plate.

"It's okay." I try to think of something deep and philosophical to say, but I've got no Yoda moments in me.

"No, it wasn't. But it's getting better. I'm getting better." She reaches out and puts her hand on top of Jess's.

I nod to keep any stupid things I might say from coming out.

"Thanks for being such a good friend to Jess," she says.

So that's what we are.

Good friends.

45

Who's in Your Herd?

Before school, I put on my *Jessica and Frankie BFF* bracelet and grab Annie's now-late Valentine's card. The one I made when Annie was *just* my former kindergarten teacher, not Dad's person. It's covered with pink feathers, silver rhinestones, and glitter. I never gave it to her on Valentine's Day, and I'm not sure I want to give it to her now. But when I see Blue Shirt Sub standing in the front of the school again, I feel a drop of missing, stuff Annie's card back into my pack, and pull out the one I made for Elliot. He left to go to his grandmother's ninetieth birthday celebration in New Jersey before my glitter fest at Mills. His card has no rhinestones, just lots of ghosts and one zombie. I put it in his locker as a post-dentist-appointment surprise. Apparently, he's starting his day getting a cavity filled.

Jess waves and smiles from her locker down the hall, the BFF bracelet dangling off her left wrist. Then Mr. Bearson calls us in. His tie is checkered with tiny elephants. "Good morning, everyone," he says as I scan the room. Shanti's doodling, Josh is writing something, and Greg is trying to get the bubble gum unstuck from his braces.

Mr. Bearson clears his throat and does a drumroll on the reading table at the front of the room. "The time has come to announce the winner of our float theme contest."

The room buzzes. Even Squirrel, the class hamster, speeds up on his wheel race to nowhere.

"While there were many creative ideas, there was one unique suggestion that stood out from the rest."

"Bet it's mine," says Caroline. "A sea animal float. Narwhals. Otters. Whales."

"Nope. I'm winning this," Raheim says. "Baseball Hall of Famers. Like Ty Cobb and Joe DiMaggio."

Mr. Bearson motions us to stop talking. "I know you're all excited."

The blueberry pancakes that Dad made me this morning flip-flop in my stomach.

"The winning theme for this year's Winter Family Festival Float is Who's in Your Herd?"

"So we're going to be like a bunch of elephants?" Shanti asks.

Mr. Bearson laughs, then shoots a broad grin in my direction. "No, elephants. Actually, the whole title is: Who's in Your Herd/Bloat/School/Murder/Dazzle/Tower? It's the perfect theme for this festival where we celebrate family."

"Still not really getting it, Mr. Bearson," Shanti says.

"Frankie, want to explain?"

The air freezes around me. I don't move. I never actually thought my idea would win. I just needed one that would keep me from being called up to Mr. Bearson's desk. I scan the room, take a deep-to-my-belly-button breath, and then share, "Those are the names of the groups that different animals live with. Like, a bloat of hippos, murder of crows, herd of elephants, school of fish, tower of giraffes, and dazzle of zebras."

I actually used dazzle *to beat Elliot in Word Play the other day.*

"So we *are* going as animals," Shanti says.

Mr. Bearson shakes his head. "No, we're going as a family. After all, that's what all these groups of animals are and that's what this festival is about—family at home and in the community."

Whoops and claps and stomps build until the room bursts with a cacophony of celebration, drowning out the few lasting mumbles of "that's not fair."

Jess gives me a thumbs-up even though her puppets seem to not understand how Fashion Trends Through the Years didn't win. I can't contain my happy dance.

"Congratulations, Frankie. You and your family will be able to ride on the float during the parade."

Ride on the float!

Woot!

With my family!

Woot!

Wait. What does that even look like?

Me, Dad, and Annie.

My family of three.

My happy dance slows.

At that moment, I realize I got what I wanted. A family for the Winter Family Festival Parade.

So why do I feel more like a lone wolf than dazzle of zebras?

46

My Dad's Person

The snow and ice crunch under my boots as I leave school. I want the yay-I-won feeling to zip up from my holey sock and flood my body, but it doesn't. It's stuck. I twirl the four-leaf clover in my pocket as I try to keep my hands from freezing on my way to Mills.

The card room smells like flowers. I'm thankful they're not pink roses.

When I walk in, Sid and Gram are holding hands. Gram pats the empty chair next to her. "Come sit."

Sid looks at me, then kisses Gram's hand. "Gonna leave you two ladies alone for a bit."

I ease into the chair. Gram smiles as she watches Sid leave the room. I wonder what's stronger, **Rule #11** or the kind of love that leads to coral lipstick, perfume, and red nail polish.

Then, as if she's flipped on her magic mind-reading powers, Gram says, "You know, loving Sid doesn't mean leaving you." She holds my hand with her soft, buttery fingers. "My heart has room to love a lot of people."

I blink back the tear that I worry might leak out.

"That's true for your dad, too." She pauses, looks into that place where most people don't see and says, "Annie's a wonderful person."

I nod.

"Your mom loved her."

I nod again. "Does Dad?"

Gram shrugs. "Don't know. I do know that his heart has lots of room, though."

"How did you find out?"

"Your dad came to me in the beginning. He wanted my blessing."

I'm not sure if I'm more surprised they had a secret that didn't include me or that Dad wanted her approval.

"And?"

"I gave it to him. Frankie, your dad loved your mom, so much. And that will never change. But he still has a lot of life to live."

The words seep deep into my skin.

"I hear he hasn't been the only one keeping secrets," she says with a laugh. "I knew you were up to something, but

Connection.com? That's priceless. Just like you, Smart Cookie." We play cards for a while, and I tell her about the float contest.

"Count me in," she says. "Maybe Sid can ride on the float with us."

I leave Mills wondering how my family now seems to include Jess's pop, and head over to meet Elliot in front of Bert's Ice Cream Shack. Even though it's freezing out, I owe him a double-scoop Oreo ice cream cone after losing the last round of Word Play. Inside, we run directly into Annie. She's with a little kid I don't recognize. Annie's hair is in a frosted silver clip, and she looks like she does every other day . . . except totally different.

Now she's my dad's person.

"Hi there," Annie says as she walks over and gives us her usual-but-now-not smile. There's no trinket or story today.

She introduces us to her niece, Mackenzie, who's visiting from Fayetteville, Pennsylvania. That's why Annie hasn't been at school. She's been showing her niece around. Elliot tells them about some famous ghost haunts close by and a really cool cemetery they should visit. I say nothing.

"What's up with you?" Elliot asks after Annie and Mackenzie find a table in the back.

Feels kind of like a trick question.

"I mean you barely said hi to Annie."

I never got to tell him about Dad and Annie. His dentist appointment ended up lasting all day. Something about an infected tooth. Sounds painful. I stare at Elliot, hoping his ghost-hunting skills help him read my thoughts.

But they don't.

"You're freaking me out. What's wrong with you?" Elliot asks. "Did something happen? I mean other than your gram and Jess's pop. I'm still processing that one."

I take in all the air I think I'll need to tell the story of Annie and the pink roses. When I'm done, Elliot's staring at Annie while his ice cream drips down the side of his cone.

"Okay, not helping," I say. "Stop staring. I don't want her to know what we're talking about, and if you bore a hole in her face with your eyes, then chances are, she'll know."

"Wow. Annie. Didn't see that coming," Elliot says. "What about your dad's profile."

"Shut it down."

"Did he find out about it?"

"I confessed. Don't worry, I left you out of the plan."

"Thanks."

"Didn't want him to kill my only ally."

"How mad was he?"

"Stop doing that thing with your eyes."

"I'm not doing it on purpose. It just happens. Like breathing." He licks the side of his cone and then stuffs the rest into his mouth. "On a scale from one to ten, how mad was he: ten—he's in the process of disowning you—one—he thought it was the best idea ever?"

"About a never-do-it-again seven."

"Not bad. I assumed a solid nine."

"I think he would've been a ten, but he'd been keeping Annie a secret from me. So not sure how angry he could really get without sounding like a total hypocrite."

"I guess. But you did make him a profile and pretend to be him to find a mom."

"For a good cause."

"True. So in a way, you succeeded. You found him a, um, you know, person." He digs in his bag and takes out a bag of beef jerky.

"How can you still be hungry?" I ask.

"Most of the day my mouth and the tip of my nose were numb," he says. Then he takes a big bite of his smoked maple beef jerky. "And I'm pretty sure the nose part was a mistake."

The smell of beef jerky bleeds everywhere. "That's the part I don't get," I say.

"Why? Are my nose and mouth still droopy from the novocaine?"

I shake my head. "No, I don't get how I could've wanted my dad to find someone before the Winter Family Festival. And he did."

"So what's the problem?"

I shrug because I honestly don't know. "Let's talk about something else. I'm sick of pink roses."

He takes a bite of the beef jerky. "Well, we could talk about Reggie and how he's trying to steal the B&B."

47

Holes

"Out with it," I say.

"Turns out Reggie wants to knock down the B&B to build his empire."

"We've been over that. He can't. We're here. Even the man who doesn't give out candy on Halloween wouldn't drive a tractor over an inn filled with people."

"Maybe not, but he's hoping it'll be empty soon."

"How?"

"I'm getting to that. First, you need to know that Reggie used to own the B&B and then, suddenly, one day, sold it to Mickey for cheap."

"Why? That doesn't sound like Reggie," I say, glancing over at Dad's Annie.

"Not sure yet. Maybe he was hoping that Mickey would keep it and then Reggie could buy it back later. But supposedly, Mickey really loved the place."

"Then why did Mickey sell it to my dad?"

"He needed the money."

I think of Mr. Cuddles at the B&B and part of me feels sad for Mickey.

"When Reggie found out that Mickey sold it to your dad, he went nuts."

"Why would Reggie care?"

"Don't know. I found emails to Mickey in those photos you took at Reggie's office. Angry emails. Then the paper trail dropped off until a few months ago."

"What happened then?" I scoop the chocolate sprinkles off the bottom of my cup.

"Reggie started some kind of development company, and he's been going around to small towns, buying up properties, with the hope of building developments, escalating prices, and selling."

"But I still don't get how he's planning on buying the B&B if my dad won't sell."

"He's driving customers away."

The sprinkles stick in my throat.

"How?"

"Cousin Mickey. Remember those brochures we saw at Mickey's house and the dates on the calendar that were circled?"

I nod. The things I didn't think were clues.

"Reggie paid him to disappear. Then started a rumor that Mickey was missing. People assumed the worst because Mickey was always in trouble. Always owing someone money."

"But I don't get how that ties to the B&B."

"This was the part that took me a while to figure out. But then I saw something similar on *The Great Ghost Pursuit* last night. Reggie pulled the classic haunting—dead owner returns to haunt his beloved old home."

"Like Beatrice Jacoby?"

Elliot nods. "Everyone in town knew how much Mickey loved the B&B. So all Reggie had to do was plant the seeds. One, Mickey owed money to some bad people. Two, Mickey was missing. Three, a ghost was seen at the B&B."

I try to take in everything that Elliot is telling me without puking my Oreo ice cream all over the table.

"Customers heard the rumors and ran. If your dad can't pay his loan, he'll have no choice but to sell or lose the property. I checked the photo of Reggie's calendar. He's got a meeting at the bank next week. It could be about the B&B."

Every empty room, cancellation, and extra batch of leftover cookies spills into my brain. But in my haze of mad, I notice Elliot's serious detective face fade into a set of sad eyes. "I guess you were right about the ghost meter after all. It's just some made-up junk science," he says.

I don't want to be right. I shake my head no. "I don't think it's really junk science. Maybe this one just has a broken part or wobbly connection."

He ponders that while he finishes the last piece of beef jerky. "Maybe. I'll inspect the meter when I get home and see if the laser's loose." He pauses and then says, "Either way, I think we need to tell your dad."

"Not yet. You said there's a meeting with the bank next week. If we get there earlier, maybe we can stop the bank from selling the loan. You know, show that Reggie manipulated this whole thing. Save the B&B."

"I just hope it's not too late."

"What do you mean?"

"If your dad's already defaulted on the loan, Frankie, we may be out of options."

48

My Plan to Fix Everything

When I get to the B&B, there's a sticky note on the front
desk with Dad's ETA. I crack open a bag of Nacho Cheese
Doritos and look around. I can't imagine living anywhere
else. This is our home. My home. I spent a whole summer
sitting on that flowery cushion by the bay window, reading
every book we keep in the lobby for guests. I learned how to
bake the best cookies ever in that oven. And I never put my
muddy sneakers in that boot bin. We can't lose this place.
I think and eat and think and eat, but no grand plan crystal-
izes. I move to the living room, and around seven, Dad joins
me, Lucy, Winston and the big bag of Doritos on the king-
size couch. Part of me wants to keep my no-secrets promise

and tell him everything about Reggie. But the other part wants to fix this. To remind him that I'm still his person.

So I tuck my secrets behind my big toe and instead tell him about the Who's in Your Herd? float and the chance to ride in the parade. Then I find my brave and my voice and ask, "Can you come?"

A yes would be a first.

A no would not be a first. But it would hurt like a first. That's the thing about nos. You never get used to them.

The pause fills the room. Lucy inches closer to the bag of Doritos and Winston until his quills prick her nose. Then Dad says, "I'm really proud of you. I wouldn't miss it," as he reaches for my orange-stained hand.

I hold on to this moment tightly.

"I asked Gram to come, too," I tell him.

"That'd be great," he says, dipping his hand into the bag of chips and pulling out a fistful.

"She wants to bring Sid."

Dad smiles and nods.

Behind him, I see Gram out the window. She's alone. I'm surprised. Sid seems to go wherever she goes these days. Except the shed. That's still just for her. And her room. That's also off-limits.

I look again. Still just Gram. But this time I see the big red door. Open.

Something clicks inside of me.

This is my chance.

My chance to fix everything.

I kiss Dad's cheek, hand him the rest of the chips, and quietly slide out the back door. I slowly creep to the maple tree and watch Gram hauling boxes in and out of the shed. Door open. Door closed. Door locked. Door open. Door closed. Door locked.

Door open. Door closed. Door *not* locked.

I wait for her to run back and bolt the door. But she doesn't. Five minutes pass. Then ten minutes. Nothing. Gram is back inside the B&B. I know she didn't mean to leave the door unlocked. I know looking inside her private space goes against **Rule #2: Stay out of the shed**. But right now, I need answers.

So I hold my breath and step inside to unearth whatever secrets are hidden behind the shed's big red door.

49

Piles

The room is bursting.

Floor to ceiling, it's full of stuff.

Piles and piles and piles of stuff.

I didn't know piles could stand this tall without tipping over. But there they are. Towers of plates and cups and saucers. Baking tins. Lamps with shades and shades without lamps. Pillows in black, white, orange, red, green, blue, gray, black, and yellow. Flashlights. Stacks of photo albums. Pots and pans. Baskets. Candles in pine scent, jasmine, vanilla, cinnamon, ocean breeze, crimson, beachfront property. Blankets. Hundreds of magazines from one, two, three, four, five, six, seven, eight years ago. Hangers. More baskets. Frames. And boxes. Lots and lots of unopened boxes.

I knew Dad promised to take care of her and her stuff. But I didn't know it was like this.

I sink onto a small box on the floor and look around.

There's no ghost here.

No Mom.

No answers.

Just stuff. Lots and lots of stuff. I survey the mounds of randomness around me. *It can't all be meaningless.* In my heart of hearts, I have to believe there's something in here that matters.

I dig through hangers, candles, old newspapers, unopened packages, dozens of glasses, and boxes and boxes of receipts and paperwork, but nothing stands out.

Part of me is mad that Gram spent so much time buried under all her things. The other part's sad that I didn't know she was hiding. I look around and wonder if Dad's right.

Maybe it's all just nothing.

Then I see it. A box that sparkles in a shaft of moonlight that's pouring in through the doorway.

A sparkly thing is not a hanger or a tin or a candle.

A sparkly thing is not junk.

A sparkly thing is not nothing.

I wedge my body between the boxes and piles, and pull out a beautiful box. It has rainbow-colored stones on the top and when I open it, music plays. I listen to "You're All I Need to Get By" by Marvin Gaye three times before I notice the handwritten letters, locket, wedding ring, snow globe, and photo at the bottom of the box. The locket has an image of Gram as a little girl on one side and a woman who I assume is her mom, my great-gram, on the other. The large photo is a picture of Gram, Mom, and me. On the back, in Mom's handwriting it says *I love you both to infinity.*

And under the words is a noseless smiley face.

50

Dear Mom

The box is *not* junk. It's a treasure. I sit and listen to the song over and over and over again as I shake the snow globe and watch fake snow cover a beautiful sandy beach. I don't realize tears are streaming down my face until the wet marks stain the letters in my hand. Slowly I open the first one.

The paper's thin and water-stained, but I immediately recognize the handwriting. It's Mom's. Gram always told me how Mom loved to write her letters. Gram says letter writing is a lost art.

Dear Mom,

Today's my wedding day, and I just wanted to tell you how excited I am to marry Brad. You don't have to worry about me.

249

We're moving but not too far. Same time zone! We're happy, and you and Dad taught me all I need to know to have a wonderful life. I love being your daughter. Love you so much.

Much love,
Meg

I only have to read the first letter to know breaking into the shed was worth every bit of trouble I may get in.

Dear Mom,

I heard from Reggie the other day. His dad died. He sounded really sad. I know they were close. His dad was a nice man. He always gave out the best Halloween candy. Remember? Extra-large chocolate bars. If you see him, be nice.
I'm excited to see you in a few weeks. Miss you.

Much love,
Meg

Extra-large chocolate bars?

Dear Mom,

Reggie's been calling a lot. He wants to know if there's any hope of us getting back together. He said he was serious about running the old B&B together. I told him he's a good friend, but I love Brad. And I'm not interested in living in an inn. Don't think he took it too well.

Miss you.

Much love,
Meg

Mom and Reggie? The B&B? This letter's dated two weeks before my parents' wedding.

Dear Mom,

Can't believe I forgot to tell you on the phone when you called, but I made these new cookies. Peanut butter oatmeal chocolate chip. Brad says they're my best yet. I can't wait to make them for you.
Miss you.

Much love,
Meg

Dear Mom,

Well, it happened. We're pregnant! With a little girl. The doctor says I'm doing well. Sending you hugs from all three of us!

Much love,
Meg

Dear Mom,

Francine May Greene is her name and she's 8 lbs, 9 ounces and as beautiful as the sun. Her face is round with honey-kissed cheeks and your bright golden-flecked, hazel eyes. I can't wait for you to meet her. I know you'll love her as much as I do. Only two weeks until your visit!

Much love,
Meg

There are thirty-four letters, and Gram saved them all.
Not junk.
Not junk.
Not junk.
Gram was right.
I tuck the letters back into the sparkly box, return the hidden treasure where I found it, and leave Mom's words in the shed.

51

One Big Fat Lie

All the pieces finally connect.

I grab two still-hot pumpkin spice muffins and meet Elliot in front of the bank.

His hair hangs in front of his eyes. "Are you sure you don't want to tell your dad?" He looks at his watch. "There's still time."

"I'm sure. I've got this," I say, ignoring the bats flying around my gut begging me to call my dad. Then I walk through the front door of the Dennisville Bank and straight into the conference room with the glass walls. When I open the door, I hear an unfamiliar voice coming from a man in a blue suit. "That is correct. Mr. Bradley Greene missed his last loan payment on the Greene Family B&B."

Am I too late?

Then a gravelly voice says, "In light of the failure to pay, continued vacancies, and increased risk to the bank, I'm prepared to buy the promissory note."

"You can't do that!" I step up to the table where the suits are sitting. "He's lying. He's a big fat liar," I say.

"Little lady, your dad failed to make his payment. That's the truth," Reggie says with a toothpick dangling from his lips.

"But that's because of you and all your lies."

"I'm not sure what you're talking about." Reggie moves closer to me. "You know, you just can't go around accusing people. That's called defamation. I could sue you," he says. Then he smiles at me.

"Actually, it's only defamation if what she says is untrue," Elliot says. I'm so thankful for his thoroughness. Elliot gives me a thumbs-up and the courage to keep going.

"You paid your cousin to get out of town, and you spread rumors that he died and that his ghost was haunting the B&B so people would stay away."

"That is a ridiculous story. Some little girl's imagination run amok." He shakes his head and turns to the suits. "I apologize for this outburst. I don't want to take up too much of your time, so let's proceed with the meeting."

"Let's," a voice from the doorway says. "And since this is still *my* business, I'm happy to be included." It's Dad. Standing next to him are Annie and Gram and Sid and Jess.

I look at Elliot. He mouths that he may have told Jess, who may have told Sid, who may have told Gram, who may have told Dad, who may have told Annie.

My body floods with something that feels like *thank you*.

I then tell the story I now know. "Reggie was in love with my mom. He bought the B&B years ago to move into it with her. But she said no. Then she married my dad." I smile at Dad, who nods encouragingly. "Reggie was heartbroken and angry and needed to dump the property. So Reggie sold the place to Mickey for cheap with the promise he'd never sell it. Years later, Mickey broke his promise. He was in debt, and my dad made him an offer. Mickey accepted, and we moved in. Reggie never forgave Mickey or my dad."

"This is absurd. You're not going to listen to some little girl's made-up tale of woes, are you?" Reggie says. But the sweat on his brow and the scowl across his face confirm my tale of woes and reveal just how worried he is that the bankers will believe me.

"Let me enlighten you with a little proof," Elliot says, smiling. He hands each suit a packet of the documents and emails that substantiate every detail of my story.

"Please don't give up on my dad." I turn and look at him. "Reggie started this. He's the reason guests canceled. He's the reason my dad couldn't pay."

Blue Suit clears his throat. "I understand and empathize with your plea, miss. But there's still the issue of the loan and the continued vacancies."

My dad shakes his head. "Francine, I love that you did all of this for me, but proving Reggie's guilt can't fix it. I still can't pay the debt right now."

"Well then, there you have it," Reggie says, standing up and moving to the front of the room.

"Sit back down, Reginald," Gram says. "I have some money tucked away from my gin winnings. It's in that blue jar in the pantry, Brad. You can use that."

"And I have a little saved for a rainy day," Sid says. "It's yours."

Maisy from the flower shop—who I didn't even see show up—pushes past Gram. "You help me all the time, Brad. Now it's our turn to help you." One by one our neighbors file into the conference room with the glass windows: Mr. Barker. Joe. Jess's mom. MaryKate. Mrs. Rudabaker. Mabel.

Our friends step up to help my dad.

To save the B&B.

And when I look around the room, I realize MaryKate was right.

My family has been here all along.

52

My Life as a Spy

After our showdown at the bank, I tell Dad I'll meet him at the B&B. I have a stop to make. The cemetery is cold today, but the sun warms my face and hands. A kind of peacefulness I haven't felt in a while settles around me. I tell Mom everything and then show her my mood ring. It's purple.

"I get it now. You can have more than one person. So take care of little Nate and Beverly and Gertrude and Markus. I'm okay. Honest. I've got my people here."

I set a bunch of wildflowers by her graveside and walk home. When I get to the B&B, I hand Dad one of the Mom cookies I made this morning and confess all the remaining secrets that have been stored behind my big toe. Unload every detail of my life as a spy—the ghost meter, Reggie's office, the clues, Dead Mickey's house, and the plans for Hogan West. I tell him about the letters and the music box in the shed, and then ask him the only question I never found an answer to.

"Why did we move here after Mom died?"

He grabs another cookie. "Mom and I had talked about moving back. Mom was worried about Gram. She had started accumulating more and more stuff. Then, when Mom died, Gram's condition deteriorated."

"How?"

"Annie called me one day. She said that Gram's landlord was threatening to evict her. I bought the B&B and the shed so she and her stuff could have a place with us. She didn't want help. Not from me or from any doctor, but she needed a home."

"Why couldn't they just give her some medicine to fix her?"

"It doesn't work that way. People like Gram need to want to get help. And Gram didn't. She just didn't see herself as having a problem that needed fixing."

"Well, whatever the reason, I'm glad we moved here. I'm glad you bought the B&B, and I'm glad Gram is with us."

"Me too, Francine."

Then he makes me promise to give up my life as a spy. That's a promise I know I can keep. I hug my dad and realize there's one more thing I need to fix.

I walk to the end of Main, across Spaulding, make a right on Broadlawn, and ring the doorbell at number 88.

The bright blue door stares back at me.

"It's me. Frankie," I call just as Annie comes to the door.

"Hello. Hello. Hello." Taco the yellow-and-green parrot lands on Annie's head, stretching out his wings and showing off the rainbow of colors underneath.

"He won't stop until you say hello," Annie tells me.

"Oh. Hello, Taco." I smile shyly. "Hi, Annie."

"Hi." She motions me into her home. There are honey-colored beads dangling between her living room and kitchen, cranberry tapestries on the walls, and cinnamon incense burning on the table. It feels like Annie.

I sink into a yellow beanbag on the floor and hand her the Valentine's card I'd made for her.

"Thank you, Frankie. It's lovely."

"Lovely. Lovely. Lovely," Taco repeats.

Annie runs her ring-laden hand across his feathers, and her silver bangles jingle against him.

"I meant to give it to you before, and then things, um—"

"Changed," she says. "Some things have. Like your dad and me not being *just* friends. But not everything has to. Like you and me. We don't have to change. I care about you. I care about your family."

"I know." For the first time in a very long time, I realize that's what Dad and I are and have always been.

A family.

Even if we can fit on a bicycle.

53

Watching Over Me

The day's finally here. The Winter Family Festival Parade. Last night left a fresh coat of snow blanketing Main Street. Our float is lined up between the seventh-grade float honoring the civil rights movement and the fifth-grade float on inventions.

"Hey, what are you guys?" It's Bailey, a fifth grader covered in silver spokes and a rubber tire from the Inventions Over Time float.

"Who's in Your Herd?" I say. I'm dressed as me: holey socks, Converse sneakers, and my green shirt with the horseshoe on it. And just before I left the house, Gram lent me Mom's silver hoops with the spot of turquoise.

Bailey makes an I-don't-get-it face.

"You know, we're a family. Like a herd of elephants, dazzle of zebras, bloat of hippos, murder of crows, pod of whales, pack of wolves, or tower of giraffes."

As she darts away to talk to the calculator, the high school band starts to play "Don't Stop Believin'." Mr. Landers, the bandleader, is a huge Journey fan.

Jess sits down next to me on the part of the float that's decorated to look like a cozy kitchen. Alongside her is Leila, her mom, Elliot, Sid, Gram, and Mabel. I invited them all to ride with me. Even asked Mrs. Rudabaker, but lunch at Mills was pepperoni pizza, so she declined. We sing together as the band plays.

I look at my watch. Ten minutes until Mayor Hartman stands on top of the large rock in the square and says the magic words: "Let the Winter Family Festival Parade commence." I bite my lip and hope the rest of my family gets here in time.

"Everyone take their places." I recognize the voice coming through the megaphone from the front of the parade. It's Elliot's mom. Ever since I can remember, she's been the voice of the parade.

Elliot leans over the edge of our float, with all his ghost hunter gear, and gives his mom a thumbs-up. He got her emergency list of nonemergency chores done early today.

I twist the four-leaf clover in my pocket.

Then I see him.

"Sorry I'm late," Dad says. "I wanted to bring some warm ones." He opens two cardboard boxes, and the smell of homemade blueberry muffins blankets the float. "Thought you guys might be hungry."

He passes the muffins around, then turns and gives me a hug.

"Who's watching the B&B?" I ask. I don't remember Dad ever being away without Gram there.

"Mr. Mendelson."

We both laugh. I bet his wife's there, too. Maybe even his brother. I envision him lining up all the books on the shelves.

I check my watch again.

"She'll be here," Dad says.

Lately, I go to Annie's house every Tuesday and Thursday after school. Turns out she plays cards. Maybe I'll even be able to beat Mabel after a few more lessons.

The floats' engines start, and the first one pulls out.

She's not here.

As the second float begins to roll, I tell myself that it's okay. It doesn't matter if she rides the family float with us or not. But in the part of my heart that hides stuff, it matters.

I hold my breath and count to twenty.

Thirty.

Sixty.

Then I see her. Annie's running as fast as she can, parrot earrings dangling in the wind. I reach for her hand and pull her onto the float.

She reaches in her pocket and hands me a dried wild-flower. Before I can weave my story, she says, "This flower has powers far greater than even the stone. It transcends time and place. Hold on to it." Then she leans over and whispers something in my ear.

I smile. "I promise. I will keep it always." My mood ring turns bright purple. In my hand, the flower feels like a sliver of what was.

I look out into the parade crowd and see Mr. Bearson handing out hot cocoa. He waves as we pass and promises me a hot cocoa with whipped cream and extra marshmallows.

With a stutter and rumble, our float takes off down the street. I've got everyone I love around me. My herd has gathered. My family is here.

Some of them are on the float.

And some are watching over me.

Macbeth—The Rap

By Frankie and Jess

Three witches tell the tale, turn courage to greed.
Ascend, Cawdor then King, oh thee.
It's yours, Macbeth. The crown, the castle with speed.
The prophecy is meant to be.

Hail Macbeth for bravery, King Duncan cries.
He shall be Thane of Cawdor now.
Prophecy realized, seeds of darkness and lies
Macbeth nor the Lady will bow.

Witches prophecy fuels the greed. Feeds the crazy.
Ends in red and daggers. All hail the king.

King Duncan to Castle Inverness tonight.
Dance, drink, and walk the greedy halls.
The crowned celebrates, wholly blind to the fight.
King's dead. Murder stains the white walls.

Witches prophecy fuels the greed. Feeds the crazy.
Ends in red and daggers. All hail the king.

Remove the sons, kill the guards, Macbeth is King.
The witches' prophecy comes true.
Scorched the snake, Banquo must die, Macbeth will sing
Witches assemble, plan anew.

Help is too late. Macbeth's crazy has grown.
Lady Macbeth is dead.
Woods move in cloak of branches, crown on loan.

Witches prophecy fuels the greed. Feeds the crazy.
Ends in red and daggers. All hail the king.

Macbeth and his Lady now colored in red.
Greed, scorn, and treachery, and hate.
Crown returned and witches' tale dead.
Story ends, prophecy of fate.

Resources Consulted

Gail Steketee, PhD, is Dean and Professor at the Boston University School of Social Work. Dr. Steketee has conducted research and taught on cognitive and behavioral treatments for obsessive compulsive disorder (OCD) and related OC-spectrum disorders, including hoarding disorder. She has been funded by the National Institute of Mental Health and by the International OCD Foundation for her research on OCD and hoarding disorder with her colleagues Dr. Randy Frost at Smith College and Dr. David Tolin at Hartford Hospital. She has published over a dozen books and 200 articles and chapters on these topics. She serves on the scientific advisory board of the International OCD Foundation, is an elected Fellow in the American Academy of Social Work and Social Welfare (AASWSW) and the current president of the Association for Behavioral and Cognitive Therapies (ABCT) for 2016–17.

Steketee, Gail, and Frost, Randy, *Stuff: Compulsive Hoarding and the Meaning of Things* (Mariner Books, 2011).

Children of Hoarders, https://www.youtube.com/watch?v=TSaxn0a1Cbk.

My Mother's Garden, documentary, Act 1 and Act 2: http://www.msnbc.com/documentaries/watch/my-mothers-garden-act-1-277091395690 and http://www.msnbc.com/documentaries/watch/my-mothers-garden-act-2-278911043859.

Acknowledgments

At the heart of Frankie's story is her love of family. That is also at the heart of mine. To me, family is everything. It is where happiness lives, sadness finds shelter, love never ends.

To my husband and my boys. James, you are my life anchor, my best friend, the love of my life. Your unconditional belief in me gives me the courage to always be me. Joshua and Gregory, your love is what fills my heart each and every day. I am so proud, grateful, lucky to be your mom. I love you all. So deeply.

To my dad, Sandy, and Gia, thank you for championing this journey, cheering me on, and loving me throughout. Always.

To my brothers and sisters (I dropped the whole "in-law" thing a long time ago) and nephews and nieces, I love you all more than you know. I am beyond grateful to share all of this with you! Thank you for always being there for me.

To my mom. No words can possibly capture the love and the loss. By the time Frankie finds her way into the world, you will have been gone twenty-two years. Too long to be without each other. But, from that place in me that remains yours forever, thank you for loving me so completely and always watching over me.

To my gram. Your mightiness remains a force that I will always try to live up to. And, Dop, you remain tucked in my heart, always grateful for your strength and love. Take care of each other up there.

As Frankie's story unfolds, she learns that if you're lucky, your family has a way of including more than just the people with whom you share a name or a room or a childhood.

So, to my editor, Jenne Abramowitz Vermeulen, thank you for being a part of my writing life and family. From the moment you shared your love of Frankie, her spunkiness, and her dedication to family, I knew that Frankie and Dad and Gram and me had found a home. Thank you for trusting and believing in me and the heart of this story. And to all those at Scholastic who edited, created, read, and helped bring Frankie to life, you have my deepest appreciation. And to Scholastic Clubs and Fairs, thanks for loving my girl, Frankie, from the start.

To my amazing agent and friend, Tricia Lawrence, I'm not sure there are words that capture the fullest extent of my gratitude. You told me I needed to write a new novel, you told me you loved it, and you told me it would find a home. And, it did. Thank you for always pushing me to be the best me and for believing in me no matter what.

To EMLA, I love sharing this road with such talented and wonderful writers. May your words always find their way onto the page.

To my Sweet Sixteens, you guys rock! So grateful our worlds connected. And a special shout-out to one Sweet Sixteen who's been equal parts champion, secret-keeper, and friend. Thanks, Victoria Coe!

I don't even want to think where this story would be without the input and guidance of Katrina Knudson, Sarah Azibo, Sarah Aronson, Joan Siff, Rena Pitasky, and Reesa Fischer. Thank you for reading early drafts, sharing your wisdom, and never letting me or the story go astray.

To my girlfriends, you are always in my heart. Thank you for being there to celebrate and encourage, to love and support. How lucky I am to have you in my life.

To Sophie McKibben, a huge thank-you for happily reading my story, loving Frankie, and sharing your Vermont wisdom. From maple syrup to blueberries on the trail to public transportation. Thank you for all of it! And to Joshua and Sophie, hugs and thanks for naming my girl Frankie!

Gail Steketee, I am grateful for your input and guidance on adult hoarding. Your information enabled Gram's situation and condition to unfold and feel authentic. I so appreciate the time taken to educate me, guide me, and read my story.

Linda Kay, I owe all my knowledge about promissory notes to you. So a hearty thank-you. And while the bank in the story is less than lovely, you and your bank are awesome!

To Jen, thanks for the Taco tales, and Raquel, who fixed up her grandmother on a dating site, thank you for sharing your story. That was the spark Frankie needed to spring to life.

I close with a special thanks to all the educators who have so graciously and warmly welcomed me into their hearts and their amazing community. Thank you for taking me in. For loving *Finding Perfect*. For believing in me. I hope you love Frankie. I like to think that she and Molly would be friends.

Grateful and honored,

Elly

ABOUT THE AUTHOR

Elly Swartz is the author of *Finding Perfect*. She loves hiking, Twizzlers, writing for kids, and anything with her family. Shortly after writing a few chapters of her first book, she found inspiration in the most unexpected place. She opened her Bazooka Joe bubble gum fortune and it read, "You have the ability to become outstanding in literature." That fortune remains tacked to the bulletin board next to her desk. Elly is a graduate of Boston University and the Georgetown University Law Center. She lives in the Boston area, is happily married with two grown sons and a beagle named Lucy. You can find out more about her at ellyswartz.com.